THE NEW BEGINNING

THE NEW BEGINNING

GILBERT W. G. CAMERON

To order additional copies of this book, contact:
Xlibris Corporation
1-800-618-969
www.Xlibris.com.au
Orders@Xlibris.com.au
501213

Novels By Gilbert W. G. Cameron.

Pandemic Series.
The New Beginning. [Volume 1 Published 2011.]
Twenty Years On. [Volume 2.] Yet to be released.

U. F. O. Series.
Second Chance. [Yet to be released.]
Outward Bound. [Yet to be released.]
The Milky Way. [Yet to be released.]

Précis About The Book

This book starts on a cold, wet, winters afternoon in London when the main character in the story goes home from work early because he is not feeling well, possibly the start of the usual winter flu. By late evening he has a raging temperature and is vomiting continuously, if he had not felt so bad and had any strength in his limbs he would have made his way to the hospital.

When he eventually wakes up he finds that his apartment is freezing cold and the central heating is not on, when he gets himself together sufficiently and finds the strength required to go outside he finds dead bodies lying on the street, vehicles are crashed all over the place with dead bodies in some of them and there is no one about anywhere, he goes back inside badly shocked and tries the telephone but it is not working and his mobile gets no answers no matter who he rings including the Police and everywhere there is a complete silence like nothing he has ever experienced before.

About The Author

Born in the Republic of Ireland in 1941, moved to Northern Ireland as a child. Left Secondary School after grade 12 and had a couple of clerical jobs, Joined the Northern Ireland Police Force, The Royal Ulster Constabulary at the age of eighteen and served during a period of the I.R.A. troubles and resigned after four years and married his present wife, has two sons. After leaving the police force he pursued a career in the field of selling which he successfully pursued until 1981 when he and his family immigrated to Australia and settled in Townsville North Queensland where the whole family became Australian Citizens in 1986. Since then he has continued his career in the sales field in the telecommunications industry until 2009 when he retired and started writing. That had always been an ambition to take up seriously. This is his fourth book that he has written and is on a subject that he has always felt deeply about most of his adult life, with the sequel still to be published.

DEDICATION

Sadly I dedicate this book to the way the World is Going at the present moment. We never seem to learn from the past, every day we help to destroy the Planet a bit more. The food we eat has so many preservatives in it that there seems to be more of them in it than the actual food itself, also we have stopped eating healthy. That would in turn help our natural immune systems, build up our immunity in our bodies and help keep it safe from viruses and germs.

CONTENTS

CHARACTERS OF BOOK THE NEW BEGINNING

BOOK 1.

{Eight bedrooms in main house.}

1. JOHN McGRATH.
Male, aged 32 years, single, worked in London as stockbroker, had girlfriend, six feet tall and fair hair, well built, no apparent overweight. FROM LONDON.

ANNE KNOBLE.
Female, aged 25 years, single, lived in Cornwall, orphan, had a boyfriend, five feet ten inches. Was a nurse and has dark brown hair and a cheery smile. FROM LONDON.

2. *RUSTY DEEMAN.*
Male, aged 47 years of age, was married, wife deceased from the epidemic, no children stockily built with a bit of a paunch but not too bad, Looked fit and used to be a factory worker. FROM CAMBRIDGE.

MARY SWARD.
Female, fifty one years of age, had been a housewife and had lived in the village of GUNTHORPE all her life, [husband deceased had been an accountant].

3. **TOM FIELDING.**

Male, thirty years of age, electrician, was single FROM WIVERTON

MARY HARRINGTON.

Female, twenty five years of age, shop assistant, single, FROM WIVERTON.

4. **BRIAN BROOKS.**

Male, Thirty eight years of age, was married, no children, carpenter by trade, FROM CAMBRIDGE.

JOANNE LANGLEY.

Female, 31 years of age, single, blonde hair [done in pony tail style], five feet seven inches in height, slim build, a friendly smile had worked as a schoolteacher. FROM HOLT.

5. **MIKE THORNTON.**

Male, school teacher, thirty three years of age, manual arts, FROM NORWICH.

ELIZABETH [Beth], FAIRWEATHER.

Female, twenty three years of age, was engaged, pharmacist, FROM NORWICH.

6. **PETER WOODS.**

Male, thirty two years of age, was single, engineer, FROM NORWICH.

JEAN THACKERY.

Female, twenty one years of age, was single, shop assistant, FROM NORWICH.

7. **HAL STERN.**

Male, twenty three years of age, third year medical student, FROM NORWICH.

ALICE BECKENTHALL.

Female, twenty five years of age, worked in a shoe shop in Cambridge, single but was engaged,, boyfriend deceased. **Was a slave in Cambridge.**

8. **Dr. PETER WILLOUBY.**

Male, forty one years of age, Doctor of medicine and surgeon, was married, no children, fair hair, FROM LONDON.

MARTHA HOPE.

Female, thirty three years of age, was married, husband and two children all deceased, was a housewife, and before that was a musician and played the violin. **Was a sex slave in Cambridge.**

9. **ADAM DUNDAS.**

Male, thirty one years of age, was single, but was going out with a girl, was a computer technician. FROM LONDON.

SARAH FYFE.

Female, twenty three years of age, single, was a receptionist in a hotel. FROM LONDON.

10. **BOB HAMMERSLEY.**

Male, Thirty five years of age, widowed, no children, Electrical Engineer. FROM MANCHESTER.

JUDY FURST.

Female, twenty eight years of age, was single, was a nurse. FROM MANCHESTER.

11. **PHILIP MITCHELL.**

Male, twenty five years of age, was single, was an Auto Mechanic. FROM MANCHESTER.

12 SUSANNE RICHARDS.

Female, twenty years of age, was single, was a computer technician. FROM MANCHESTER.

SINGLE ROOMS.

13. ROB BARNES.

Male, 19 years of age, spiky red hair, freckles on his face and had worked on his fathers mixed farm. FROM HOLT.

14. ROSEMARY BECKWORTH.

Female, sixteen years of age, had been at school, parents had died in the pandemic. FROM GUNTHORPE

15. ARTHUR GROUNDWATER.

Male, forty years of age, mathematician from Manchester University. FROM MANCHESTER.

16. ARBARA BAILEY.

Female, thirty years of age, worked in safari park, was single, FROM WOLVERHAMPTON.

DOUBLE ROOMS.

17. LUKE FADER.

Male, nineteen years of age, single, third year apprentice in carpentry, parents deceased.

18. JASON TONNER.

Male, twenty seven years of age, single, handy man, did odd jobs and small house renovations. FROM WIVETON.

&

19. DON WHITESIDE.

Male, forty two years of age, was married, and had two boys, all deceased, an engineer FROM LONDON

20. JOSEPH EPTON.

Male, fifty one years of age, novelist, single, had retired from London to the country for the peace and quite to write historic novels. FROM BERMINGHAM.

FOUR BUNK ROOMS.

21. PAUL STERN.

Male, ten years of age, spiky red hair, parents both deceased, FROM LONDON.

22. PHILLIP FIELDHOUSE'

Male, fifteen years of age, parents both deceased FROM MANCHESTER.

23. AUSTIN GOODWIN.

Male, eleven years of age, parents deceased FROM MANCHESTER.

24. TOD WESTON.

Male, twelve years of age, parents deceased,FROM WOLVERHAMPTON.

25. LISA BELLINGTON.

Female, twelve years of age, schoolgirl, lived in village with her parents and three siblings, all deceased. FROM BINGHAM.

26. POH-WANG.

Female child, twelve years of age, both parents and siblings all deceased still fairly well traumatised. UNKNOWN WHERE SHE IF FROM, picked up along the road side.

27. JUNE DURHAM.

Female, 10 years of age, schoolgirl, Parents and three siblings all deceased. **Was a slave in Cambridge.**

COMMITTED SUICIDE.

28. MAY FORRESTER.

Female, 19 years of age, single, parents deceased, was at university doing social studies and was from Cambridge where she had been held as a slave.

CHAPTER 1

THE END OF EVERYTHING.

It was a dull, wet, cold winters afternoon early in February and John McGrath was headed home from his work early because he was feeling so miserable. He called into the nearest pharmacy to get some cold and flu capsules and aspirin to dose him self along with a hot drink when he got home and before he went to bed that night. He had all the usual flu symptoms, blocked nose, sore throat, a splitting headache, aching bones and he felt miserable and sorry for himself or as his girlfriend would say he was being a typical male. He dosed himself with his medications and drank heaps of water as he had a raging thirst as well just to cap everything else off. As the evening wore on he kept feeling worse and worse until if he had the strength to get out of bed he would have gone to the doctors or the hospital, but he was feeling so bad and did not even have the strength to go to the kitchen to get a glass of water for his raging thirst. Eventually as the night wore on he lapsed into unconsciousness with a raging fever and the perspiration just poured from his body in streams until the bedclothes he lay on were soaked all the way through to the mattress.

The fever broke and he gradually regained consciousness and some time later after lying there in an exhausted daze for some time he managed to get enough energy to drag him self to the kitchen for what was the number one priority, a drink of water.

The apartment was freezing cold and the radiators were not working and there did not seem to be any power on in the apartment either. "Christ there must have been a blown fuse while I was out of it." He muttered to himself as he searched for something to eat as he realized that he was starving on top of everything else. He peered at his watch and suddenly realised that he must have been lying unconscious on his bed for five days by the date on his watch, if it was correct, no wonder he was starving and thirsty, he headed for a shower to try and rid himself of all the sweat on his body but had to suffer a cold one as the water was cold, so the shower did not last too long but at least he felt cleaner.

That must have been some dose that I caught he thought to himself, and I seem to have lost a ton of weight as well, my ribs are sticking out and the flesh is hanging on me and I am as weak as a newborn kitten.

He got dressed and even though he was feeling very weak he decided to walk down to the corner shop and get a newspaper to see what had been going on while he was out of it for five days. When he opened his front door the first thing he saw was a car had mounted the pavement practically at his own doorstep and the driver was hanging out of the car and was obviously dead. As the shock from seeing that he lifted his gaze to take in the street and everywhere he looked all he saw were crashed vehicles and people laying all over the place and none were moving or crying for help. "My God." He exclaimed aloud. "What the hell has happened?" He noticed newspapers lying on the ground and picked up a few of them and scanned the headlines.

"Planes fall out of the sky because their pilots die at the controls, Pandemic rages out of control across the Planet, seems to be one hundred percent fatal, millions die all over the world. Authorities helpless." The shock of the situation makes him head to the only security that he knows, his apartment and he staggers rather than runs back to it and slams the door behind him.

After a few moments he gathers himself enough to pick up the phone so as to try to ring the police but it does not work, he then tries his mobile but no matter who he tries to ring the number just rings out., none of his friends or workmates answer. "I can't be the only person left alive." He exclaims aloud, but as time goes on and none of his friends answer his calls despair sets in and he sits down and sobs until the tears run down his face "What can I do?" he says to himself talking out loud just so he can hear his own voice and to break the silence. The silence starts to get to him even though it is no worse than the normal silence in his apartment when he is on his own but he suddenly has become conscious of it, he decides to leave the apartment again and even though he has no car of his own he can not see why he should not take the one from outside in the street, after all the person in the car can not use it themselves and will not complain and at least the keys are in the ignitions.

He takes off and just drives not caring where he was going, just driving, he knows that he is acting crazy but he just can not make any sense out of the situation. Everywhere he looks all he can see are bodies lying everywhere, their eyes are all open and they have crazy expressions on their faces ranging from fear to just plain crazy, every where he looks all he can see are newspapers lying all over the place, he had never seen so much paper blowing around the streets. Every street that he drove down there were houses burnt out and in some cases they were still burning. In one instance he could see that a plane had crashed into an office building and it was still a raging inferno and would obviously continue to burn and sweep everything before it until the fire reached a point that there was a sufficient gap between the buildings that it could not cross over. No where was there any sign of life until he was passing a park and saw movement, he immediately turned into the park looking for the movement that he thought he had seen, after searching for nearly thirty minutes he was just going to give up thinking it was all in his imagination when a Labrador dog ran out of the bushes with a human arm in its mouth which it dropped when it saw him in the car and growled and showed its teeth before gathering up its prize and running off into more shrubs and bushes. The situation made him break down again and he sobbed in self pity for a good ten minutes before he managed to take a hold of himself, the next thing that he saw were a couple of African lions walking through the park as if they owned it and a couple of monkeys swinging through the trees obviously some poor zoo keeper knowing that he was dying and the world population with him decided to open all the zoo cages at the London Zoo with the animals in them to give them a chance to survive and not starve to death. He decided that discretion was the better part of valour and stayed in the car and continued his meandering search back on the road.

He decided to find a hotel close to where he was as it was too late to make his way back to his apartment across the city because he seemed to have driven a fair distance in his meanderings. He went to the closest hotel that he could find and went up to the reception desk and lifted a key from the key board and made his way over to the stairs and up to the first floor and tried the key in the lock of the door to room two which was what it said on the key ring.

He opened the bedroom door and entered. It was a normal lower price range hotel bedroom with a bed, chair, a drawer unit, bar fridge TV and had a double bed and also an en-suite off the bedroom. There was a radio built into the bedside clock and he spent about ten minutes going over all the wave bands trying to get a live station but to no avail. John went over to the bar fridge and with a half laugh that was more a sob he opened the fridge and muttered to himself. "At least I won't have to worry about the prices for the mini bar." He lifted out a bottle of beer and two miniatures of whiskey and threw himself down on the bed and opened the beer which he drank straight back because he still had this abnormal thirst and then sloshed the two miniatures into a glass. He drank the spirits and then fell asleep lying on top of the bed because he just did not have either the strength or the will power to get undressed and under the bed clothes

The next morning he awoke and found that the room temperature during the night must have woken him enough to make him want to climb under the doona for some heat.
He snacked on some of the chocolate bars that were in the bar fridge and then went downstairs and out on to the street to the vehicle that he had commandeered the day before, he decided to resume his searching.

An hour later when driving down a street he found himself passing a car showroom for new range rovers and said to himself. "Why not." Stopping the car he went inside and after searching around for a while he found a board in one of the offices with bunches of keys on it and carried it out to the showroom and tried them in the vehicle that he had chosen until he found a set that fitted the ignition of that vehicle and managed to start it, switching it off he then went into an accessory shop attached to the showroom and found some camping gear and loaded up the rear of the 4 X 4 with a sleeping bag and half a dozen car rugs and a couple of water containers, a battery lamp and a box of batteries that fitted it, a mentholated spirit camping stove five empty petrol jerry cans and most important of all a portable generator. He drove the car out of the showroom and as he started off down the street he again saw a pack of dogs feeding on bodies and they barked at him as he drove past.

"I am going to have to do something about them before to long, after I get petrol and some groceries." He muttered aloud to himself. The first priority was to find a petrol station, he just kept driving until he came across one, he drove onto the forecourt and pulled up beside the pumps. Now he wondered how do I get petrol when there is no electricity. He went into the station through the already open door and after rummaging around he found a crank handle and instructions with it telling one how to operate the pumps in an emergency if there was no power to pump the petrol out of the pumps. He went over to the pump beside his vehicle and found the crank hole behind a sliding metal disc on the side of the pump, he put the end of the crank into the hole and after putting the nozzle of the hose into the petrol tank on the 4 X 4 he started winding the handle and was pleased to find the gauge on the pump showed he was getting petrol, he filled the car's tank and after taking a short rest from the exercise he also filled all the jerry cans he had put on the roof rack. Right now for some food, just down the street he found a supermarket and again the doors were not locked he just had to slide the automatic doors to one side which was easy as there was no power in them trying to stop him and he filled up a couple of shopping trolleys and some tins of soft drinks and groceries, mostly all either tinned stuff or freeze dried packets. He decided next to go to his girl friends address to see if she was there, after about twenty minutes of driving through the debris filled streets that were filled with cars and busses just stopped everywhere, he drew up outside her flat and went inside. He had a key to the front door and with fear and trepidation he opened the door and went inside but she was not there, he did not know whether to be relieved or not but he just felt empty, she or her body could be anywhere.

When he went back outside he had to make a run for the car because another pack of dogs started running towards him. "That's it I will have to find a means of protecting myself." He stopped at the first public telephone box he came across and grabbed the directory from it and looked up gun shops and drove to the nearest one, when he arrived at the shop he found it was locked up tighter than Fort Knox with steel shutters and padlocks and a metal front door. He decided that it would take too long and too much effort to try and break into it so he went looking for another one. After a fifteen minute drive he drew up outside another sports and gun shop which when he tried the door he found it was unlocked and he went inside. The first thing he saw was a body draped over the counter, obviously it was the owner who had collapsed in his premises.

There were plenty of weapons in the cabinets. He decided to help himself to two of everything. Automatic rifles, repeating shotguns, a couple of large hunting knives and sheaths, plenty of ammunition for the rifles and shotgun cartridges. Also there was a locked gun cabinet which when he found the keys and opened he found that it was full of revolvers and automatic hand guns, keeping to the same calibre ammunition he took two revolvers, forty fives, two automatics that had laser sights attached to them and also found holsters for them, he immediately put one of the automatics on to his belt and he also took a smaller F. N. Browning automatic, a thirty two which he was able to find a shoulder holster for and all the ammunition for the hand weapons that he could find. Feeling a bit more secure in himself he loaded all his possessions into the back of the land cruiser that was looking decidedly full with everything he had gathered together.

Right he thought as the breeze brought to him the smell of all the decomposing bodies lying all over the city, it is time I got out of the city before I catch some horrendous disease and that would be ironic the last man on the planet dies of the plague or some such thing. So I will need some time to allow all the bodies to decompose or get eaten by the wild dog packs or the carnivores from the zoo and for all the fires to burn themselves out.

CHAPTER 2

LEAVING LONDON CITY BEHIND.

It was cold and damp on the dawn of a new day and the sun peeked out from behind a cloud in the grey sky when John set off the next morning on his trip to leave London and all the corpses and potential disease behind him and go into the country until it was safe enough to return to forage which could take up to a year.

He decided to head sort of north west to Norfolk which was an area of small towns like Kings Lynn and small Villages and Hamlets and was only about one hundred and twelve miles from London. He hoped he could find somewhere there where he could make a life for himself and wait until the environment adjusted to the changes that were about to happen with no human being to maintain the roads and infrastructure.

After threading his way in and out of all the vehicles lying abandoned just about everywhere one was to look and having to backtrack because some of the streets were blocked where fires had made some of the buildings collapse into the streets and in other areas where the fires still burned out of control. He had just turned down a side street that ran along side a park when he saw a large pack of dogs that were obviously stalking something, he pulled up the vehicle to see what it was they were after and saw them trying to surround a

German shepherd which was obviously not one of the pack and was defying the pack and refusing to be moved away from something he seemed to be standing over. As he got closer he saw it was a human body lying on the ground and the shepherd was straddling it. He drew up beside the dogs who were not to be put off what ever they had intended to do for they started to circle the vehicle and growling and showing their teeth and making rushes at the car and then backing off to circle him again. He decided that enough was enough and took out one of the forty five revolvers and wound down the drivers window and fired at a particularly large mastiff that was one of the most aggressive and fired at it but missed, he fired twice more and on the last shot managed to nick the dog on its back and between the gunshots and the yelp of pain from the mastiff the pack took off. "It looks like I am going to have to get some practice in before I am much older." He muttered aloud.

The shepherd that had attracted his attention had not run off it still stayed standing over what he now saw was the corpse of a young woman and obviously the dogs mistress and the dog had stayed loyal and was trying to protect her body from the marauding dog packs.

He called to the dog and tried to placate it and reached into the back of the rover for a tin of meat that he opened and threw to the dog who sniffed it and promptly gulped it down in two mouthfuls, he opened another tin of meat and threw it to the dog as well saying. "You deserve it for your loyalty, good dog! Will you be friendly?" He got out of the vehicle and the dog rose up on to its feet from where it was lying beside the body and let out a low growl that seemed to say be careful and don't push your luck too far and the hackles on the back of its neck rose up slightly as a warning also. He crouched down on to his knees after first getting another tin of meat from the back of the car and held it out to the dog in his hand who after looking at him and the meat for a couple of minutes decide that he did not present too much of a threat and slowly made his way over to John and slowly took the lump of spam out of his hand and literally swallowed it in one gulp, when John looked close at the dog he could see that its ribs were showing through its coat, the dog obviously had not eaten for some time. John decide that one more tin of meat was all that he was going to feed the dog for the moment or it would probably vomit the lot back up again, he got a dish from the back of the vehicle and filled it with water and put it down in front of the dog who promptly lapped up the lot without stopping and then went into a spasm of coughing for about two minutes from drinking too quickly after not having had a drink for some time, this time when he spoke to the dog he got a tentative wag of its tail. "What am I going to do not only with you but your mistress as well he mused."

He went round to the back of the four by four and found a spade that he had thrown in there and decided to bury the body in a nearby flower bed as the soil would be easier to dig. He dug a shallow grave and watched attentively by the dog he dragged the girls body over to the hole he had dug and rolled the body into the grave and covered it up with the soil that he had dug out of the grave and patted it down while all the time his every move was watched by the dog. He had found that its name was Max from a tag on its collar. "Do you want to come with me Max?" He asked the dog and held open the passenger side door to see if it would make a move to join him.

Immediately the dog jumped in and onto the passenger seat and settled down, "Your mistress obviously had you very well trained, well at least you will be good company and I can talk to you and not just myself from now on." He said to the dog. He noticed the dog pack were starting to come back again having gotten over their fright from the gunshots. He decide this time he would make a better job of it than he had before and got out one of the automatic rifles and using the vehicle bonnet as a gun rest he picked out one of the larger dogs and lined it up in his sights and shot it with the first bullet and then moved the sights on to another and shot it too and also a third one until the dogs had scampered out of sight into the bushes and he had no more targets.

He got back into the vehicle and put it into gear and drove back to the path he had driven down from the road and headed back to the main road with his companion happily sitting beside him. He had only driven a couple of hundred yards when he had to brake suddenly when unexpectedly a figure ran out of a side street right in front of him and when he braked they fell in front of the vehicle as the car hit the figure with a bang. The dog barked and John said "My God it is someone else alive, if I have not just killed them." Although his speed was not fast as he was being careful He quickly got out of the vehicle and ran round to the front and found a person moaning and lying on their face on the road.

"Are you all right." He shouted as he bent down to roll the person over on to their back and immediately found himself looking at what was obviously a girl, filthy dirty and unwashed hair. She opened her eyes and said. "Are you real?"

John replied by asking. "Are you badly hurt?"

"No I don't think so only a couple of bruises I think." as she tried to sit up and groaned with the effort. " I heard the gun shots and I have been running trying to get here before you went away as I thought I was the only person left alive in the world. Do you know what happened, why is everyone dead? Has there been a war or what happened?"

John hunkered down beside where she was lying on the road and tried to explain what he knew which was little enough and what he had deducted. He helped her to her feet and said. "Firstly I think you need to clean yourself up a bit and also examine the new bruises that I have just given you. Do you live close by?'

"No I was in town from Cornwall visiting my boy friend when I got sick, he went out to get help and I never saw him again and when I woke up everything was like it is now."

"Right there is a ladies outfitters and dress shop across the street, I suggest you go in to it and help yourself to several changes of clothes including jeans and an anorak jacket etc, whatever you need and then go over to that hotel and have a shower and examine your cuts and scrapes to see how you are and to clean any dirt out of them and Max and I will wait outside the bedroom door for you to finish, we won't go away, don't worry." He added seeing the look of horror on her face at the thought of being alone again. "By the way my name is John McGrath and this is Max, we had just found each other before I knocked you down."

"Thank you, my name is Anne Knoble, I won't be long." She got to her feet properly and set off across the road to the shop he had indicated and appeared about twenty minutes later laden down with shopping bags and headed into the hotel just down the street. John and the dog followed her across the road into the hotel and soon found her by following the sound of running water from a shower, coming from a bedroom with the door propped open. He and the dog waited outside and after about thirty minutes she appeared in a white blouse and jeans with a dark blue anorak over the top and her dark brown hair obviously freshly washed. She had three carry bags from the shop clutched in her hands, "Right I am ready and that feels a lot better." she remarked as she tried to put on a brave smile on her face.

"Right." said John indicating that he would help carry her shopping bags. "We can talk in the car." He said as he started for the stairs down to the ground floor with her trailing along behind.

They got in the car where Max was waiting for them without incident and John started the engine and put it into gear and started off.
"I am sorry for nearly running over you!" said John as a way of starting the conversation rolling.

"No, no not at all it was all my fault running out like that onto the road without looking where I was going, I had heard the gun shots so I knew that there was at least someone left alive other than myself and then I heard the car start up and I was afraid that I would miss you, that you would have driven away before I got there, I was desperate and staggering around in a daze and just not able to take it all in, you are the first person that I have seen since I woke up in Greg's flat, that was my boy friend that I had come up to London to visit, he went out to get me some medicine when I took ill and I have not seen him again and I think that was several days ago, I was unconscious, when I came too I staggered outside and all I have seen since are dead bodies lying everywhere."

"In my case I was unconscious for five days lying on my bed in my apartment and like you when I came too all I could see were all the dead bodies lying all over the place and the crashed vehicles. From what I have been able to find out from newspaper headlines was that there was some sort of pandenemic which has swept the whole world and has killed off about ninety nine per cent of the worlds population, so to all intents and purposes it is the end of the world as we know it and only a few people with a natural immunity have manage to survive. I have decided to leave London because of the dog packs which are getting dangerous and also the rotting corpses are going to be a big problem with disease especially when the rats decide to come out of hiding in the sewers etc, when they find that there are no more humans to try and get rid of them, you are more than welcome to come along with me, I am thinking of heading out into the countryside north of Cambridge, possibly Norfolk, Kings Lynn or one of the small hamlets or villages in that area until things here take there course which will probably take at least a year and it is safer to return and then I would try and get a lorry and return and forage for supplies to help with survival."

There was silence for a moment while Anne tried to take in what John had said and then she replied. "I would not mind if you will take me with you I think you have possible worked out the only viable solution to our problem, I wonder will we come across any more people."

What Anne had just said reminded John of something and he drove the vehicle into the side of the kerb. "That reminds me I want you to wear this all the time, even when you go to the toilet." He replied as he took off the shoulder holster rig and handed it to her. "Believe it or not you must not trust anyone you meet for the first time until they prove themselves to you that they can be trusted just because ninety nine per cent of the population has died off does not mean that all the bad ones are gone and only the good remain, it just does not work like that, this situation can bring out the worst in people, such as rape, pillaging trying to set themselves up as dictators etc especially when there is no one to hold them accountable for their actions and punish them accordingly. Also we are going to have to find a spot soon to practice with these weapons, I have already found out that I am useless with the hand guns but I can just about pass with the rifles and we need to be proficient with both also there is this hunting knife I want you again to wear it at all times strapped to your thigh and I have a rifle in the back for you as well which is not to heavy and I am sure you will be able to manage it quite well, I want you again to carry it at all times when you move around outdoors because the dog packs will try to sneak up on you without any warning and spring on you to get you down on to the ground so you must be careful at all times and learn to read the environment."

He started up the vehicle again and continued to head north towards their ultimate destination, even as they got out into the countryside there were still bodies to be seen in parked and crashed cars and lying along the roadside. It was obvious that no matter where they decided to settle there would be bodies that they were going to have to dispose of away from where they ultimately decided to live.

They drove for another two hours and then decided to stop when they could find a shop that sold groceries so as to get some food for themselves, not long after they stopped outside a grocery shop in a village and went in to explore and found that it was well stocked so they helped themselves to what they wanted in the tinned line as all the fresh meats etc. had already spoiled then John went down the street about fifty yards and into a pub and got some tins of lager and brought them back to the vehicle and Anne had already put the tinned goods into the back along with some tins of soft drinks. They then went back inside the shop again to grab some food to eat now and so as not to touch what they had put into the vehicle. Max was given the usual couple of tins of meat and Anne found a couple of large dog dishes which she appropriated for Max, one for his water and one for his food, she also grabbed half a dozen bottles of water for the dog, again they did not want to touch what water John had already put into the back of the car. They set off again and after a while they reached the outskirts of Cambridge and decided to stop there for the night. They found a pub and went inside to have a look except for a couple of corpses in the lounge bar it appeared to be empty.

John soon removed the two corpses and carried them outside into the yard at the side of the building and Anne went into the kitchen to see what she could find and Max padded in after her and sat down at her feet while she worked, she heard John shouting to her from outside and she rushed out to see what was wrong. "What is it she shouted as she came out the side door into the yard?"

"Sorry." John replied I did not mean to upset you I just thought it would be a good chance to try out the guns and see how we do, I never thought when I shouted for you it was completely thoughtless. I see you did what I asked anyway and brought the rifle with you, I have set up some bottles as targets and I thought this was as good a place as anywhere to try out our skills or lack of them as the case may be, I see Max has set himself the task of looking out for you, I notice he does not go to far from your side, which is good that he has adopted you, it gives you that extra bit of security if I am not about. Do you want to go first or will I?"

"No you first said Anne with a laugh, I have never fired a gun in my life so I know that I will be bad and I want to see what expertise that I have to beat, it may not be too high a standard, I hope."

John stepped up to a line he had drawn in the dust on the ground with his toe and raised the 45 automatic gun up to shoulder level and aimed at a bottle amidst the row he had put on top of some beer barrels and fired the gun which went off with a loud bang and nothing else seemed to happen, certainly there was no explosion of glass from a shattered bottle. Red faced he tried again and they both this time saw some wooden splinters from the side of the barrel splatter where the bullet had obviously hit. He gritted his teeth and tried again and continued until he had emptied the gun and the only results were a couple more lots of splinters from the barrel but no hits on the bottles.

Anne walked over to him and keeping her face dead straight she said "I see what you mean about it being hard and that you were not a very good shot," let me have a try and see if I can do anything. She stood up to the mark and fired her first shot and a bottle exploded. She jumped in the air in delight and John had the good grace to look pleased for her and suggested she try again, she again stood at the line and fired until the gun was empty and scored two more hits.

"You certainly seem to have the knack of it." Said John red faced as he moved over to the line again to once more try his luck.

"I am no expert but try stroking the trigger instead of pulling it, that is what they always say in any movies that I have seen." Remarked Anne. "Mind you I am no expert."

John thought to himself I have nothing to lose I may as well try it. So once again he stood at the mark and raised the gun and carefully took aim and held his breath and tried the technique of stroking the trigger and not pulling it and fired the gun and was rewarded with a bottle exploding. The only thing was that he was too embarrassed to admit that the bottle he aimed at was next to the one he hit. He again raised the gun and fired and kept firing until once more he ran out of bullets, this time his total was three bottles.

They kept up the practice for the next hour and both steadily improved but Anne was still obviously the best shot of the two of them. They decide to have one more round each and John was just steadying up his aim to fire when they heard a voice speak from behind them.
"I would keep up the practice if I were you as you obviously need it." They both spun round at the sound of the voice. A man in his late forties or early fifties was standing in the entrance to the yard with a smile on his face.

"Hi! I am Rusty Deeman, I heard all the shooting and decided to investigate as it looked like I was no longer the last man on Earth."

Anne let out a small scream and John with a startled look on his face went forward to greet the new arrival with a smile and said. "Delighted to meet you I am John and this is Anne and we are from London and are on our way out into the countryside to get away from all the corpses until things settle down."

"Yes it is getting a bit hard on the nose around here, I was wondering myself what I could do about it. As I said I heard your shooting and came a running, I had literally thought that I was the last man alive and was getting very depressed."

John and Anne both said. "Come inside with us we were just getting ready to make a meal, you can swap stories with us while I see what I can find to eat in this place." Anne indicated the side door to the pub and motioned for Rusty to precede them inside.

Once inside Anne stated that she would see what there was to eat while the two men sat down on the bar stools with a beer each and they could talk and she could put in her two cents worth from behind the bar while she was looking for food. Rusty's story was very much like their own, about becoming seriously ill and falling unconscious and waking up after a few days to the world as it was now and thinking that he was the last person alive on the planet.

John explained that they were hoping to make their way into Norfolk around the Kings Lynn area and sit it out for at least a year until the scavengers and nature had done their bit to rid the countryside of all the corpses and possible disease and asked Rusty if he would care to join them if he wanted to and he would be most welcome. Anne from the kitchen area as she had said was listening in to the conversation and shouted from the kitchen that she agreed if he would like to come along.

Rusty with an embarrassed smile on his face said that he would love to come with them as they had what sounded like a good plan of action.

"Also believe it or not I am quite a good shot with either a hand gun or rifle, it stems from my time in the Territorials, although I have not acquired any weapons yet."

"Fine." Replied John. "Before we move on tomorrow we can go looking for a gun shop and get you fitted out with what ever is necessary for your protection, by the way have you acquired a vehicle yet?"

"No I have just been using whatever was at hand and dumping it when it ran out of petrol"

"Okay that is something else we need to do is find a car showrooms and get you a 4 X 4 possibly the same as ours as later it makes sense to have our vehicles all the same for the reason of repairs and spare parts, and maybe Anne we should think about getting you one too."

"Fine whatever you say is okay with me."

For the time being they decided that it would be better and safer if they spent the night all together in the lounge bar on one of their comfortable big chairs with a nice log fire burning in the hearth. They retired early after a meal of scrambled eggs and tinned spaghetti.

The next morning they were up early and after a pot of coffee had been consumed they went out on the scrounge with their shopping list. The first thing they went looking for was a car show rooms that sold Land Rovers, after a look in the yellow pages they had made a list of garages and found one that sold Land Rovers, a gun shop, supermarket and clothing shops and each did their shopping and loaded up all three of the vehicles with as much as they could fit in, Max as usual never left Anne's side and gave a growl to warn them if any dogs came too close for his liking.

Eventually they had all the things that they could think of packed into the vehicles and set off on their journey again.

After driving for an hour they started to come to a lot of small hamlets and villages and started to seriously look for one that suited them.

After an hour and a half of driving from one village to the next they eventually found a small hamlet called Hunworth and it had a river called the Glaven running alongside it and it had a watermill at one end of the village that the two men decided after examining it that it could be made serviceable again as it looked is if someone recently had spent time and money on it, there was a couple of pubs in the village although one was more of an eatery than a pub it was called the Honey Bell and also a small grocery shop come post office. The closest town of note seemed to be called Holt and was not to far away and it looked like it would have just about anything that they may require.

They found a large house built off flint beside the watermill and decided to move in there, it had five bedrooms and a large study and a newly renovated kitchen and a good sized larder and a large storeroom and all the other necessities of life. They did the usual thing and checked for corpses first but found none, thank God, and started carrying in all their gear that they had accumulated on their trip down from London or in Rusty's case from Cambridge and putting it in the bed rooms that they had chosen for themselves. By the time they had put everything away in the bedrooms and the food stuff in the larder and some into the storeroom where they had multiples of an item it was getting quite dark and they lit up some candles that they had acquired and then went about preparing their first meal in their new home. Rusty peeled some potatoes and John looked out a couple of tins of vegetables and helped Anne with the main course that turned out to be a conglomeration of tinned meats and of course the usual couple of tins of meat for Max. They even found a couple of bottles of wine, one red and one white which helped the meal along nicely and then they barred and bolted the doors and windows and retired to their respective rooms and of course Max was along with Anne. Before heading to bed they had decided that the first thing on the agenda in the morning was to search the village for bodies and to dispose of them somewhere that would not cause them any problems later on.

CHAPTER 3

SETTLING IN THE VILLAGE.

The next morning after they had breakfast they decided to look around the village and see if they could come up with a trailer to hitch on the back of one of the Range Rovers and they could put the bodies in it and use it to transport them out of the village to wherever they were going to dump them. After look around behind several of the houses they found what they were looking for, a trailer that was suitable to hitch on behind their vehicles. They had managed to find overalls, surgical masks and gloves on their last foraging expedition before they had found the village they had taken over knowing that they were going to require them for this unpleasant task.

They decide to start next door to the house that they had made into a communal house for them selves to live in. They found one body of an elderly woman and they loaded her into the trailer and moved to the next house, they found two bodies in it and on to the next and so on down the street. Meanwhile Anne had been out in one of the other vehicles looking for a spot to dump the bodies and had found a disused flint quarry about three miles outside the village on the road to Holt which was the nearest small town about five miles up the same road from the village.

By the time she returned to the village the two men had managed to fill up the trailer with bodies so they followed her out to the dump site and pronounced it as more than suitable for the job. They returned to the village and continued with the unpleasant job of gathering up the bodies from the village.

It was hard backbreaking work carrying bodies and some of them were not light, at lunch time they took a break and went back to their house and Anne made some sandwiches and they had a beer each. It was hard backbreaking work carrying bodies and some of them were not too light. They continued working all afternoon until dusk, finding bodies and carrying them out to the trailer and then transporting them to the dump.

They decided then to call a break for the day. They reckoned that they had found most of the ones in the village, there were only a few houses left to search in the village itself and a couple of houses that were out on the outskirts. They returned to their house and lit the log fire which helped cheer them up as it was a depressing job that they had been doing all day, the only good thing if you could call it that was that there had only been a couple of children's bodies in the houses that they had searched so far, everyone seemed to be in the latter part of their lives or probably retired.

After they had made a meal for themselves they decided that on the next day they would finish the job in hand and then they would give each house a good search for any food or anything else that they thought may be useful to them and bring it all back to their house. They locked up and headed off to bed.

The next morning when they came downstairs Max was grumbling in his throat and kept looking at the door. Rusty looked out the window and saw a couple of hungry looking dogs wandering around so they got their guns and went outside, the dogs which seemed to be part of a pack of about a dozen of various breeds growled and put their hackles up. Rusty immediately shot the largest one and the others joined in as best as they could. After the firing stopped they found that they had killed four of them and it looked like the rest of the pack had run along with a couple that may have been injured. John said to the others. "It looks like we are going to have to discourage the dogs from this area by shooting every time we see a dog whether it is threatening us or not, they will soon get the message and give us a wide birth. Rusty agreed and Anne said "Do we have to? All right I can see by your faces we will have to." They threw the bodies of the dead dogs into the trailer and continued on with their grizzly search of the last of the village and outskirts, by lunch time they reckoned that they had finished, and after having something to eat they started on their scavenger hunt for food and anything else that they may find a use for, candles and kerosene being high on the list. As the day wore on they had each made about four trips with the three cars full of goods and food. They decided that they would call it a day and returned home.

That night as they sat around the fire they discussed the way things were going for them and what the future might hold for them.

Anne as ever was the practical one where food and clothes were concerned. "I think we need to make a trip into Holt and stock up on food as well as what we are gathering here in the village and we should try and get some seeds for planting for vegetables and stockpile them as we will eventually run out of food from the shops."

"Yes I agree." Replied John. "I vote that we finish the job here in the village first and then we do a trip to Holt and see what we can find."

Rusty chimed in with the suggestion that they only take one car and see if they can acquire a small panel truck in Holt and a couple more generators. They started making out a list of what they thought they might require, and worked at it until bedtime. The next morning after a quick breakfast of tinned fruit and coffee the three of them got into John's Range Rover and started off for Holt the nearest township to their residence. After thirty minutes of careful driving because they did not know the roads and did not want to smash into a car abandoned in the middle of the road. The trip was uneventful and the road was clear all the way to Holt. When they got out of the vehicle they put on their surgical masks although they did nothing to help the smell, which seemed to permutate everywhere but they knew that as the day wore on they would get used to it. They made their way first of all to the dealership for Range Rovers and managed to find a new double axel four by four which suited their purposes, it would do instead of a small truck and again kept their vehicles all the same make.

Anne and Max went off in the Range Rover with her share of the shopping list and promised to be careful, Rusty had at the same time as they picked up the small truck had also obtained another Range Rover to add to their collection and he went looking for his share of the list. John had a sudden thought when he looked at his list and noticed that they had made no provision for books or pharmacy items, so he decided to start with the pharmaceuticals as there was a large chemists shop right beside where he was standing. He went inside and lifted everything that he thought they may require as time went by from bandages, patent medicines, drugs, and anything that looked useful, including several large packets of toilet rolls which he lifted with a smile, and thought to himself now that those were very necessary, as he came out to load his scavenging proceeds he noticed several dogs had started to move in closer to him so he unlimbered the rifle and managed to shoot a couple before the rest fled round the closest corner, he also heard Rusty shooting off a few shots and knew that some more dogs had bitten the dust to use an old cowboy metaphor. He decide to look for a good sized book shop and remembered that he had seen one somewhere around where Anne was doing her shopping, so he climbed aboard the vehicle and put it into gear and moved off in her direction.

Anne meanwhile had made her way to a large local supermarket that they had managed to find using a local map that they had managed to acquire and started loading the car trunk with shopping trolleys full of tinned and packaged food, Max sat on the pavement outside the front door and kept watch. She was down the back of the supermarket and had found boxes of candles and was putting them into her shopping cart when she heard the front door bang and Max started doing his nut and was throwing himself at the door which had obviously closed with him outside and he did not like it. As she made her way down an isle she heard a noise behind her and as she spun round she caught a glimpse of a man standing behind her as he swung his fist and caught her on the side of the face and knocked her to the ground, he immediately jumped on her and grabbed her rifle that she was madly scrabbling for where she had dropped it when he hit her.

"Now we don't need that now do we? Or this either." as he relieved her of her .32 from the shoulder holster. "What do you want she cried out at him, still trying to get over the punch in the face that he had given her by way of an introduction.

He leered at her from a face covered in stubble as he obviously had not shaved for some time and he smelled so badly she found her self gagging as his smell wafted over her from where he straddled her waist. "I thought I was never going to get some tail ever again and here you turn up all pretty and done up just like a Christmas tree. You and I are going to have some fun together and then I will take you back to where I have made myself comfortable and we will have more fun." He reached down and started to unzip the front of his trousers and at the same time he was trying to get her jeans down over her hips and was trying to grope her. While this was going on she was screaming at the top of her voice and struggling to get him off her but he was too strong and he was laughing all the time and saying, in a crazy manner with spittle's running down his chin from his mouth. "Go for it bitch there is no one to hear you, or did you not know that everyone else is dead, and again he laughed.

She was trying to get at her knife which was strapped to her right thigh but she was half lying on her side and could not get at it and all the time Max was outside and trying to get in to her and going mad. She was struggling that hard that he got annoyed at her and hit her again on the face a couple of times, by now her screams had turned into sobs and she was whining from the pain of where he head hit her and also from terror.

Suddenly without any warning Max was all over them both and was trying to rip out the mans face with his teeth and he appeared to have him by the ear and was in the process of ripping it off, he rolled off her as he fought with Max and he was screaming and she could hear the fear in his voice as Max looked as if he was getting the best of him, then he managed to get himself partially clear and swung Max at the shelving and groped for a gun he had stuck into his waist band.

A voice shouted out "I would not do that if I were you, Max no, stop, sit, that is a good dog." Max immediately sat down with his lower jaw on his front paws and stared at the man and continued to growl and snarl at him. "If you reach for that gun again your are dead." came John's voice as he shouted at the individual in a tone of voice that brooked no argument.

"I was not doing her any harm, we were just getting to know each other. I did not know she was taken,. You can have her he whined.

Meanwhile Anne was gathering herself together, and sobbing with relief at being rescued in the nick of time.

As she started to calm down John asked. "Are you all right, did he rape you?"

"No thank God but if you had not come when you did." and a sob caught in her throat

"You can thank Max I was down the street and I saw him going crazy and I knew that something was wrong, when I reached the shop and opened the door Max just plunged in, there was no stopping him and I was hot on his heels and you know the rest.

As for this maggot we have to sort him out!"

The man by this time knew he was in deep trouble and no amount of talking was going to get him out of it. "What are you going to do to me." He whined

"There is only one thing we can do with you." said John, walking up to the man and putting his gun to his head.

: "You can't kill me, I will move out of town away from you."

John said okay but I can do this and he again put his gun up against the side of his head and pulled the trigger and shot him dead without any further ado.

"If I had let him go he would have come back and cause trouble in the future and we might not be so lucky the next time and there are no Goal's anymore or police men."

Anne gave a scream at the unexpectedness of the action and then broke down crying on Johns shoulder. After a few minutes the sobs died away and she sobbed. "Thanks again John, lets get on with our jobs!"

"Are you sure you are up to it, that looks like you are going to have a nasty bruise on your cheek and eye, why don't you go and sit in the truck and I can finish up in here."

"No thanks all the same I think I will feel better if I find something to do, rather than sit in the truck and feel sorry for myself. Do you know what I mean?"

"Yes of course I do but just take it easy, no one is judging you or has a clock on you." The two of them then went about gathering up from the list everything that they required plus other things that they thought of when they saw them on the shelves. Anne put the items into the trolley and John wheeled the trolley outside to the truck and unloaded them into the back of it, where possible Anne chose cartons of goods rather than separate cans, but when she came across an item on the list she took all of it that there was to be seen. Max did not leave her side for long at any time and if he went to the end of an isle he looked around and then came straight back to her side. she kept giving him plenty of praise and even opened a tin of his favourite food Spam and fed it to him, it did not last two seconds but was gulped down in one mouthful, John came back from one of his trips at that point and laughed and went over and patted him. "You are going to be spoilt from now on I think." They finished up in the supermarket and decided to go to a bookshop and then find a gun shop to pick up more ammunition.

They found quite a large bookshop on the main street and went inside.

"What are you after John, anything in particular?"

"Yes I want to get an up to date copy of Encyclopaedia Britannica, A large dictionary, and an Engineering Electrical Britannica."

They started searching and Anne was the first to strike gold. "Over here John." She was right there was a full set of the encyclopaedia that he was looking for on the shelf for 2009 and beside it was a seven language dictionary by the same publisher, after a further search they found the other books that they required. They carried them out to the truck and Range Rover and then went in search of a gun shop which they found and were lucky in that it wasn't locked up, barred and bolted and they were able to grab all the ammunition that they required and also more handguns and several more rifles including one snipers rifle and shotguns. "I think that will do us, I suppose we should go and look for Rusty and see how he got on." Anne agreed and they both went outside to the two vehicles carrying the last of their acquisitions from the gun shop.

Max as usual hopped in first along with Anne the minute the door was opened in the Range Rover and John had climbed into the truck. As time had passed Ann's manner had cheered up with having something to take her mind of her terrible experience earlier on.

They made their way to the rendezvous arranged before hand and found Rusty waiting for them and there were two other people standing beside him a woman and a young male teenager from what they could see at first glance.

"Good to see you Rusty. I see you have managed to find some company while we have been away." Said John by way of a friendly greeting so as to put the two new people at their ease as he could see they were a bit apprehensive in their stance."

Rusty immediately saw the damage to Anne's face as by this time the bruising on her cheek and the shiner on her eye had both come up a treat to behold. "What on earth happened to you Anne?" He voiced in concern as he immediately came over to her.

Anne immediately started to shed a couple of tears as the situation came back to her in all its horror, brought on by the sympathy in Rusty's voice.

John quickly explained what had happened and finished by saying that he had shot and killed the man involved as he had come on the scene just in the nick of time, brought there by Max going off his block outside the supermarket and he had gathered that something was wrong and had come at a run to arrive just in time as things were getting very serious. Rusty was most sympathetic and at the same time was trying to introduce his two companions.

"Sorry people." He said to the two of them. "This is Joanne Langley and this is Rob Barnes, they have been together for the last few days, they heard my gunshots at a pack of dogs that were giving me a tough time of it and were being persistent and they came looking for me and luckily found me." The woman was in her early thirties and had long blonde hair tied up in a pony tail and was about five feet seven and slim build and when introduced she had a ready smile, the boy was approximately eighteen or nineteen years of age and well built and had a mop of spiky, unruly red hair and his face was covered in freckles. John immediately approached them with his hand out and a big smile lighting up his face and said. "We are really glad to meet you both and it is good to see that you appear unhurt and non the worse for wear considering that I know what you both must have gone through in the last week or so, I hope you will both join our small group, I am sure you will find it to be to your benefit, if you don't like the way we live you will be welcome to go on your way and see if you can find anything else more suited to you and we would send you off with plenty of supplies and weapons so that you would be able to take care of yourselves."

Joanne spoke up. "We would love to join you, we had already discussed this possible situation after we had recovered from the sickness and decided that it would be better and safer if we joined a group of people, that is why when we heard the gunshots we came looking for you. The bloke you had the unfortunate run in with, we saw him a couple of days ago and he had tried to get us to join him, but we ran off because of his threatening attitude and he looked untrustworthy."

The young man Rob. Spoke up and smiled a broad smile that lit up his face and also highlighted his youth, we would love to join you, it seems like you are getting yourselves all organised."

John said. "That is settled then but as you can see all our vehicles are pretty well stuffed with supplies I think it would not be a bad idea to acquire another vehicle, can either of you drive?" they both spoke up and said that they could drive. "Fine we will go back to the showroom and get another Range Rover if they have left any there, we are keeping all our vehicles the same so as to make servicing and repairs easier and the keeping of some spare parts."

They made their way back to the showrooms and drove another Range Rover outside and then decided that they may as was well fill it with supplies too, as there was no point in going home with a car empty and the space going to waste, so back they went to the supermarket and they quickly filled that to and then started for home.

When they arrived at the village they drew up outside the large house that they had made in to their headquarters and started to unload their goods. John passed the remark that they would have to put up some shelving in the room that they had made into a storeroom or they would never be able to find anything. After two hours hard work with them all helping carry the supplies inside they had finally emptied the four vehicles.

When they were all inside and seated at the large kitchen table and drinks in front of each of them to their taste and the two newcomers had been allocated bedrooms and were settled in there. John remarked that they had omitted to acquire some clothes and shoes and work boots for the two new recruits but that could be taken care of tomorrow. Rusty brought up the subject of keeping the dog packs out of the village and he had made a trip to a hardware shop and also a farm equipment store and had seen plenty of fencing that they should get along with a couple of electrified fencing kits and batteries and that would help keep them away from the village. And also they needed fencing that the dog packs could not get through to put some cattle or, pigs and sheep behind to keep them safe or they would all soon be wiped out, also it would be nice occasionally to have some fresh meat instead of tinned stuff all the time, not that he wasn't grateful for what appeared on his plate at meal times but fresh is still fresh especially a nice big steak occasionally.

They all agreed and decided that would have to be their next priority along with shelving for the storerooms. It was decided with all agreeing that tomorrow they would each drive a vehicle and again load up with supplies as much as they could fit into the Rovers and one Rover and the double axel truck would go to the hardware shop and the farm supplies and the rest of them would again visit the supermarket and gun shops, also the clothing shops and anything else that they could think of. After they had eaten and before they all went to bed John issued the two newcomers with a handgun, rifle and shotgun each and ammunition for them and also the usual large hunting knife, it turned out that Rob had used both rifle and shotgun but not a revolver and Joanne had never fired a weapon in her life and would require some lessons as soon as possible.

CHAPTER 4

BUILDING THE VILLAGE DEFENCES.

Everyone was up the next morning about seven am, and down for breakfast which the two girls had prepared. There were fried eggs from the supermarket that were still fresh and a tin of ham had been opened and sliced and fried in the pan along with onions and coffee had been brewed for those that liked it and a bottle of cola for Rob who said that was his preference, although the others kidded him about it until his face went the same colour as his hair in embarrassment until Joanne laughingly told them to stop it and eat their food.

After breakfast they all set off in convoy to Holt and their assigned shopping lists, they arrived in about twenty minutes and split up. When the men arrived at the hardware shop they loaded up with timber shelving and nails and all the tools that they might require either now or in the future including a petrol driven post hole digger. Then they made their way to the farm supply business and firstly loaded the truck with as much of the rolls of fencing wire that they could get on the truck along with picket fencing posts and also timber posts and wire and anything that would be required to attach the fencing to the posts and also half a dozen electrified fencing kits and spades and shovels and pick axes and anything that they thought they might need to help with the immediate jobs they had planned.

They did not take a lot of time getting what they wanted then they decided they would go and look for the other half of their party. It did not take to long to find them, they were in the clothing shop getting themselves outfitted having already filled most of their three vehicles with another assortment of good from the supermarket and also another trip to the gun shop and camping store.

The two men entered the shop and called out to the two women and young Rob who they saw had posted himself at a shop counter and was keeping watch with his rifle at the ready and Max was sitting beside him as watchful as ever though they did get a tail wagged at them when they entered the store.

The two women showed the men what they had acquired and asked did it meet with their approval, although in the same breath they were told, so sad to bad if it didn't.

After a few more minutes they finished up and made their way to the shoe department and tried on some shoes and work boots which were duly added to their bundles of acquired clothing and they helped to carry it all outside to the vehicles. They decide that was enough for this trip and headed home.

Again once the reached home they unloaded everything and stacked the hardware outside and everything else was brought inside and put away. The first thing that the three men did was head to the storeroom and put together the shelving that was required in both there and the larder and then left the women to pack everything away and make some sort of sense from the piles of stuff scattered on the floor in the rooms and outside in the corridors. The two older men went outside to look at where they were going to fence the village and asked Rob if he wouldn't mind carrying the boxes of tins into the girls to put away as it would help speed things up.

The two men spent the rest of the day walking around the village and drawing sketches of where they wanted to put up fencing. One good thing was that one side of the village was bounded by the river Glaven and that acted as a secure boundary on that side and there was a bridge over the river at one end of the village and that also made their job a lot easier.

The next four weeks were spent in building and putting up a secure boundary around the complete village and a secure gate across the bridge at one end and another secure gate at the other end of the village street and also more trips back into Holt and a couple of other neighbouring small towns for more fencing and picket posts. And more electric fence kits as they were determined to have a secure fence line completely surrounding the village. They also started in putting a secure fence round a couple of large fields adjacent to the village that they wanted to put livestock in. Anywhere they found cattle either dairy cattle or beef cattle or sheep or pigs they started to round them up if any were found and putting them into the fields that they had started to secure. It took another four weeks of hard work by the men and also the women who had come out to help and hopefully get the job done more quickly. Eventually after ten weeks in total all the fencing around the village and the fields for the livestock were completely secured. And they had managed to round up six dairy cattle and ten beef cattle of varying ages and a flock of twenty sheep and half a dozen pigs, four of which were sows and the other two were bores. The girls one day disappeared and were very secretive about what they were up to and came home with twenty hens of various breeds that they had managed to catch and of course the inevitable one cockerel to do his part for the future.

By this time John and Anne had paired off and were sleeping in the one bedroom and were very happy about the situation. Every time they left the village they made a point of filling up the vehicle with supplies that they managed to scavenge, so much so that the store rooms in the house had been filled up long ago and they had to make another house into a store for the supplies that they were still gathering up at every opportunity. The two women had started baking bread and it was a very welcome addition to their meal times. Young Rob had asked if he could look after the animals and the farm side of their livelihood as he was happy working with animals and knew what he was doing. This more than suited the other two men as they freely confessed that they knew nothing about farming at all.

As usual when there was any major decision to be made they all sat down at the table and discussed it and then made a joint decision with majority ruling. It was the twenty first of June and they were holding their monthly meeting where everything that needed to be discussed was put on the agenda and had time allocated to discussing it. The first thing on the agenda was put there by one of the girls about establishing a vegetable garden and using some of the seeds that they had managed to accumulate on their savaging trips, this was discussed and it was agreed on unamously and it was decided that they would cordon off and fence an area for this purpose as close to the main house as possible. The next thing was that John had put on the agenda that he and Ann would like to move into one of the other free cottages in the village as they were now a couple and it would also free up another bedroom in the main headquarters house for any one else that may join them, Rusty and Mary Sward also said they would like to move into a separate house for themselves as they had found that they were getting on well together, this again would mean that there were now three bedrooms free in the main house. This again was agreed upon by everyone. The next important item on the agenda was the defence of the village in case of an attack by an outside gang that might want to take over what they had worked and slaved over for themselves, this led to a lot of discussion but was agreed upon eventually, the next item on the agenda was to find if there was anyone else out there that might want to join them. If there were other people out there it was felt that they would be aware of their group by now because of the amount of supplies that were going missing on a daily basis from the surrounding countryside on their scavenging trips. Again a vote was taken and it was decided that John and Anne would take a trip out into the countryside for a week and see if they could find anyone and make contact with them and to take each case from there on its own merits. After that there were only a couple of small items that needed clarified and they soon got through them and the meeting was ended and they all decided as had become their habit to have a couple of beers after the meeting before everyone headed to their beds.

The next day John and Anne packed up one of the Range Rovers with the gear that they thought they may need for the week away including their weapons and enough food and water for two days as they thought that they would live off the land rather than deplete any of their stores. Rusty and Rob along with Joanne promised to take care of themselves and told the other two to do the same, they departed to Holt as their first destination. That morning about ten am.

They arrived at Holt without any problems and drove to the main street and parked themselves and got out of the vehicle and split themselves up into two different positions that would allow them to give cover to each other. Anne then at a signal from John fired six evenly spaced shots into the air from her rifle and then waited five minutes and did the same again. They did this for an hour but no one appeared so they decided that that they did not think that there was anyone else alive in the town. They decided to try Letheringsett next and drove there and did the same routine again after an hour they decided to move on so then tried Sharrington then Thornage Stody and Briston. They decide to call it a day in Briston and went into the village Pub and stayed the night there and had a meal in their room of stewed meat heated on the methylated spirit stove and tinned fruit. The next morning they decided to continue as they had done on the previous day and just continue to widen the circle around Hunworth and use it as their base. They decided to try Melton, Briningham, Gunthorpe, Hindringham, Bale and Field Dalling in that order.

They had no luck in Melton, Briningham and then arrived into Gunthorpe and did the same process there and after the third volley of shots a woman's voice called out to them from the security of a nearby house. "What do you want?" Anne called back. "We are looking for anyone else that is alive and we have been searching the villages nearby, we do not mean you any harm come out and talk to us!" A few moments later the front door of the house that the woman had spoken from opened and a woman in he fifties appeared and came out on to the street and slowly approached Anne, she stopped about ten feet away from her and said. "What do you want with me?" "We have a small community over in one of the nearby villages and wondered if you would like to join us there, it is safe from the dog packs or anything else that you may be afraid of, would you like to join us or would you rather stay here on your own?"

"Do you really mean what you say, what will you make me do for you?"
"Nobody will force you to do anything against your will and if you don't like it you are free to move on anytime, mind you everyone does pull together for the good of us all and we take turns doing chores and things that have to be done like cooking, feeding the animals or whatever needs to be done, would you like to join us?"

"I am not on my own there is a young girl of about fifteen with me as well."

"She can come as well and the same conditions apply to her."

The woman then smiled and turned and spoke over her shoulder in the direction of the house and a young girl appeared after she was told by the older woman that it was all right, it was safe to come out. She hesitantly walked over to Anne and the woman like a bird ready to spring into the air and take flight. Anne sat down on her hunkers and said. "Do you mind if my companion comes over to join us." indicating John.

"No that is all right." Replied the woman who then introduced herself as Mary Sward and the young girl as Rosemary Beckworth. "We have been living here since the Death! We have not see anyone else in all that time, although we have heard gun shots on a couple of times, I suppose that was you trying to attract attention.

We would love to come with you and live with other people again like the old days."

The two took them down the street to where they had been living and they all went inside out of the sun which was starting to warm up now that it was June. Mary made a cup of tea on an old range stove and Rosemary brought it over to the table.
They were pathetically grateful for the company and the offer to let them join their small community. John explained that there were only the two of them plus three others back at the village which were made up of one woman one

man and a young boy of nineteen. And what they would do would be to take the two of them over to the village the next day and drop them off and they would continue with their hunt for survivors.

Anne and John stayed with the two new additions that night in their house and the next morning they packed up a suitcase each and headed off back to Hunworth to drop off the two new recruits. They arrived at the Glaven bridge security gate that was at the opposite end of the village from the Mill and honked their horn and Max came lolloping up to greet them along with Rusty and Joanne.

"We have made a couple of new friends that we have brought along to stay with us." Said John to Joanne who arrived first with Max. and Rusty trailing along behind.

Joanne unlocked the padlocks on the gate and swung it open, immediately Max was over to greet Anne, standing up on his hind legs and licking her face. Anne turned to the newcomers. "Don't be put off by Max he will lick you to death." John and Anne made small talk for a few moments than said. "We had better be off. Joanne will take care of you and help you settle in." smilingly said Anne as she turned back to their vehicle and waved as she got in to the cab and John set off once again on their quest to try and find other people alive in the immediate area.

They once again decided to start an arc search pattern starting with Swanton Novers and from there on to Thursford, Hindringham, Binham, Langham, Glandford and on to Wiveton. That gave them a list of seven more small villages and hamlets to search before working their way over to some of the larger towns in the area.

Their first three places visited on the list all drew blanks and they decide to visit one more hamlet before stopping for lunch. They drove into the outskirts of Binham and immediately saw two people, a young girl who appeared to be about twelve or thirteen and a man who appeared to be in his fifties come out of a cottage and waved at them to stop their vehicle.

"I thought we were the only two people left alive. My name is Joseph Epton and this is my very good friend Lisa Bellington who used to live down the street from me and was already a friend and we sort of found each other after the sickness and found that everyone else had perished. Are there many more people left alive? Where are you from? What happened? There is no radio or TV and there are corpses everywhere!"

"Hang on, Hang on, one question at a time." Said John with a smile and then introduced himself and Anne. He went on to explain things as they understood them and explained what he and Anne were doing on their trip and invited them to join their group at Hunworth.

"We have nothing here, I am sure that I speak for both of us when I say we would be delighted to join your community."
The young girl put her hand trustingly into the older mans hand and smiled and murmured in a quite voice. "That's okay."

John asked them if they could make their own way over to Hunworth or did they need a lift.

Joseph said no they would be okay as there was nothing to keep them here and they would go over on their bikes, all that they needed to take with them were clothes and shoes and he might take a couple of books with him including the one he had been working on before the Death. They parted and went their separate way's.

The next place they called on was Langham and they had no luck there then on to Glandford. Their last place to call on for the day was Wiveton. Once again they drove onto what appeared to be the main street and they sat down together and John started the familiar routine of firing six shots and waiting for five minutes and then repeating the procedure. They had only been there for fifteen minutes when a man in his twenties hailed them from a bedroom window in a house across the street from them.

"Who are you, what do you want? Don't try anything as we have you covered with our weapons."

John stood up and called back. "We come in peace, we have been searching the area to see if there were any more survivors."
The man called back. "Don't move I will be right down." He appeared at the doorway to the street from the house he was in along with two other people, a man and woman both in their late twenties.

"Hi I am Tom Fielding and this is Mary Harrington and Jason Tonner, both from around this area. I went out in my truck and did what you are doing, looking for people. I searched all the way up the coast line from Weybourne toHolkham and I only found the two of them."

John explained about their situation and that with the three of them they now totalled twelve people found in the area including him self. He invited the three of them to join their group and explained what they had done up to now and that they would be cutting short this trip as Jason had already explored the region and other than filling up their vehicle with as many supplies as they could pack in as they never returned to their place with out gathering up a many supplies as possible before returning.

The three newcomers had a quick discussion between themselves and agreed that they would like to join the group based at Hunworth. They would just gather up their few possessions first and then go with John and Anne in their truck and help gather up various supplies that they thought may be required in the future including as much food as possible. By the middle of the afternoon they had all finished scavenging and loaded up the two vehicles and headed off to Hunworth.

It was just turning dusk when they arrived at the gate into Hunworth and honked the horn and Rusty came running up the street to the gate to let them in.

"Hi folks." He said and grinned at them. "See you managed to gather up a few more recruits John."

"Yes we will head over to the main house and do the introductions there." he replied back.

They drew the two vehicles up to the front door of the main house and John ushered the new arrivals inside to the main living room and found most of their group sitting there, the only ones missing were Mary Sward and young Lisa and Rosemary who were in the kitchen judging by the sound of voices coming from there. John introduced the three newcomers and asked if there was anything new since they had been away for the last couple of days.

He was told that Rusty and Mary had moved out of the main house into one of the cottages together and other than that there was no other news. Tom Fielding one of the new comers spoke up and said that he and Mary Harrington had been getting on well together and could they move into one of the spare houses in the village rather than living in the main house.

It was immediately agreed upon as it would also make more room at the main house as they were fast running out of room and it would mean that there was just enough room for the remaining six people to have a bedroom each in the main house without anyone having to double up anywhere.

Everyone talked for a while and then the three newcomers were shown to their accommodation and everyone headed for their respective beds.

The next day it was decided at breakfast when everyone was present that John, Rusty, Jason and Tom would go to the mill and look at what would need to be done to make it viable again for grinding corn and also to see if it was possible to hook up a system to generate electricity from the water wheel as well.

Rob, now known to everyone as Bobbie was off to the farm and Joseph Epton along with young Rosemary who had accompanied him and Mary Sward and

Mary Harrington had retired to the kitchen to prepare food for everyone for lunch and the evening meal.

After lunch John and Tom Fielding decided to go into Kings Lynn to pick up some supplies that the reckoned they would need at the Mill and also to stock up on a few other items required for the farm and they also had a list that everyone had added to if they thought of anything that was needed. After driving for an hour they were on the outskirts of Kings Lynn and made their way to the farm produce merchant first and gathered up the few items that Bobbie had asked for, and then on to the largest hardware shop in the town. On the way there John had stopped at a bookshop and picked up about a dozen books on D.I.Y from carpentry, electrical and anything else that he could find that he thought was relevant. Once at the hardware they gathered up reels of electrical wire and connectors and electrical tools and anything that Tom Fielding thought may be useful either now or in the future. Then they went to a clothing shop and picked up a few items that were on the list and then on to the closest supermarket and filled up every space that was left in the two vehicles with food items tinned and otherwise. It was late afternoon by the time they decided that they had better start for home.

On the way home a couple of wild dog packs followed them for a while before they gave up the chase because of the speed they were doing in the vehicles. John made a mental note to beef up their defences at the village to keep them and anyone else out side their perimeter. By the time they arrived home it was completely dark and they were driving on headlights. When they arrived at the bridge gate they found Joseph sitting on a tree stump smoking his pipe and waiting patiently for them to arrive home, he let them in and securely locked the gate after they had passed through, they made their way to the house and went inside to be greeted by a nice warm fire burning in the grate and the girls were setting the table for dinner. They were asked how they had managed and it was decided to leave the unpacking of the vehicles until the morning. Over the next three weeks the five newcomers settled in with everyone else very well and everyone seemed to be pulling together and there did not seem to be any friction at this stage. They spent a lot of time beefing up the security of their defences and adding another couple of electric fence packages to their existing systems and strengthening the fences themselves so that they could not be pushed over or crawled under by either animals or humans.

For the last couple of weeks Tom Fielding and Jason Tonner had been working at the mill to see if they could rig up a source of electricity. They did have several petrol driven generators but were not using them at the moment because they did not want to become dependant on them because one day they knew that petrol was going to become scarce. They had managed to rig up a small generator at the Mill and that was actually producing electricity and had led wiring over to the headquarters house and were getting enough power to run a couple of lights and a fridge. All their cooking was done on a Rayburn Range stove that was fuelled by wood and also provided their hot water. This old fashioned stove had made a return in popularity over the last ten years or so and thank goodness for that as it was one less problem to have to solve.

All in all they were comfortable and had most of the amenities that they had all grown up with. It just meant that they had a wood gathering chore that had to be kept up so as to have an over supply rather than let it run down.

Joanne Langley along with Rosemary Beckworth brought up a subject that no one had thought of up to now and that was an alternative form of transport. Both of them had ridden horses for most of their lives and actually had owned horses at the time of the Death. Joanne had been the one to first bring up the subject.

"The day is going to arrive when we find it hard to get a hold of any petrol, if not us then any children that we have. I just think it would be a good idea to catch some horses that are already domesticated and bring them back here and we all start to learn how to ride them, also at the moment they are already trained and will not have forgotten all their training and we do not have the hard task of breaking them in to riding or the plough or pulling a cart, even though some time has passed they won't have forgotten everything they have been taught, so the task will be that much more easy for us."

After a discussion everyone agreed with her suggestion and it was decided to try the next day to find some horses, starting with Joanne's horse and then Rosemary's. As Holt was furthest away they thought it was a good idea to try there for Joanne's horse first to see if it was still alive and then they could try Gunthorpe for Rosemary's horse.

They decided that the first thing that had to be done the next morning before going off after the horses was to prepare a field for the horses to graze in and also a shed and a couple of lean toos' for shade for the animals and have water laid on for them. They had already ear marked a field next to where the livestock were kept as useful for a possible expansion for them and it already had a large barn with divisions already erected inside that divided into several stalls that would be perfect for the horses and all they had to do was put up secure fencing and erect a couple of places with shade for the animals and find a couple of water troughs and install them along with a water source

Over the next six weeks they all worked hard to have the field made ready for its new occupants, by the time it was eventually made ready everyone was getting impatient and could hardly wait to see some horses in the field. They decided that night that they had done everything was done that could be done including the gathering of hay oats and meal from the farm produce merchant they had previously visited. They had cleaned up the barn and done any repairs that had needed to be done and built hay racks in the stalls and led water into each of the stalls and also built a secure lean too so as to be able to store more hay when they acquired it.

The next day the two girls along with John, Anne, Mary and Jason set off in three vehicles to look for the horses and left Rusty in charge of the village.

The three vehicles arrived into Holt and first thing they did was to make their usual foray into the shops for supplies and food and also to fill up the vehicles with petrol and also any jerry cans they could find as well, then on to where Joanne had kept her horse.

They arrived at the riding school and made their way up the driveway and immediately saw some horses galloping in a nearby field, the minute they saw the vehicles they immediately came over to the fence to see if it was anyone they knew. Other than they all looked like they could do with a good brush and comb they all looked fairly healthy and glad to see them. Joanne said her horse was usually kept in another paddock round the other side of the stables. They went round there and Joanne skidded her vehicle to a stop and dived out of it and across the driveway and up and over a gate and straight over to a horse who came galloping up to her and whined in pleasure as she burst into tears and hugged the animal which was taller than her and obviously very glad to see her. The others stood back and gave her room as she was obviously very upset as well as glad to see the animal. While they were standing there they heard a bark from a dog and a black and white collie came charging round the side of the house towards them. The two men, John and Jason went for their guns and were preparing to fire when the dog skidded to a halt and crouched down and wagged its tail furiously at them obviously delighted to see them and just as obviously meant them no harm.

Joanne called out and shouted. No! Don't shoot that's Jessie! The dog belongs to the stables and is very friendly."

John then turned to his truck and fished out a tin of meat and held it out to the dog who literally crept across the ground on its belly and hungrily took the spam and gulped it down in on go. And whined in pleasure when John patted its side and tummy when it rolled over onto its back. "It looks like we have acquired another dog.' By this time Anne had come over and was making a great fuss of the animal that was sniffing her hands and lower legs as she could obviously smell Max off her.

They rest of the party decided to explore the stables and look and see what they could salvage out of the stables for their own use. Young Rosemary was the one with the knowledge and she soon started to take down tackle from where it hung on the walls. Joanne was useless as she was still outside talking to her companion a young mare as it turned out and only four years old. The others started to pack the vehicles with everything from saddles, bits, reins, blankets and horse liniments and brushes and combs and they also found traces and reins for putting a horse into a cart.

They went back outside and found a double horse float and attached it to one of the Range Rovers. Joanne was able to have her horse go into the float without any bother and they then asked her opinion which other horse should they take with them and she picked out a fairly large sturdy horse that appeared to be friendly and said it would do very nicely for one of the men to ride. She also went hunting other types of saddles that she said were working saddles and found two of them. They all agreed that they were delighted on how easy it was so far and they were also as the saying went waiting for the other shoe to drop. They set off for Gunthorpe where Rosemary was from and arrived at the farm / stables where she had kept her horse, on arrival her horse was not to be found although there were about nine other horses alive and the bodies of from what they could see four dead animals spread over a couple of fields, they looked like they had been savaged by dogs.

Rosemary shed a few tears for her horse that they could not find and then went about looking for a couple of other horses to take with them. One for her and another spare one as well, they reckoned that they would require about six riding horses and one that could pull a plough and a couple that could be used to pull carts both passenger and a farm cart for carrying goods. They picked out two riding horses, two fairly young mares that were fairly sturdy and looked like they would be happy enough to carry anyone on them and put them into the other horse float that they had picked up in Holt at the other stables and started off for home.

They arrive back at the village and were met at the gate by young Rob who gave his usual big grin and opened the gate for them. They made their way into the village and with everyone excitedly watching them put the four horses into the paddock they had prepared for them and brought them over to one of the horse troughs closest to the barn and let them drink to their hearts content and then the two horsy girls as everyone called them went and got some oats for them and meal which they made into a mash and fed the four horses, putting the food into two food troughs they had also made for them. Everyone then left the field with the exception of Joanne and Rosemary who were lost in their own world and had big happy smiles on their faces.

Everyone else started to unpack the usual supplies they had brought back with them and piled all the horse tackle at the gate for the two girls to pack away where ever they wanted it, they also left a couple of lanterns for them in case the needed them if they were not finished when it got dark.

The next morning they were awakened by Rob sounding the alarm they had fixed up some weeks ago. When they rushed outside the found Rob staring at the gate at a vehicle sitting outside it and what looked like a couple of men standing beside it cradling guns in their arms. John told the others to go back inside and try and cover him while he walked up to the gate to see who was there.

As he got closer he discovered that two men both in their late thirties or early forties standing beside their Toyota Land Cruiser one black and one Caucasian and what looked like a young girl sitting inside the vehicle. "Good day gents he greeted them, what can we do for you?"

What looked like the older of the two men replied. "How are you? We arrived last night and saw your lights on in a couple of the houses and decided it would be better to wait for daylight before approaching you so as to avoid any mistakes."

"Yes that was a good idea, my name is John McGrath and I am one of several people who have banded together here for mutual convenience and protection."

"My name is, Don Whiteside and this is Brian Brooks and in the vehicle is little Poh Wang she is only twelve years of age and we have sort of met and stuck together, I am from London and Brian is from Cambridge and little Poh is from a roadside along the way and we have sort of adopted her. We had an idea there were some people around here from the way the food supplies have been salvaged. So we have been searching for you for the best part of a week. Not to beat about the bush too much, we would like to join you, we would work for our living and help in any way we can, it would be nice to see other people and Poh needs to see other women and children."

"I can see no reason why you can not join us, there is still room and it is good to see other people and hopefully they can bring other skills into the community."

"Thank I am an engineer and Brian is a carpenter and Poh she is just a nice kid." He smiled as he said the latter.

John thought to himself why not, they appear to be okay and their job categories are what we need, he smiled at the two men and said "Why not, welcome to Hunworth, come in and join us for breakfast."

The gate was opened and their land cruiser was driven through and directed down to the main house where it drew up and the three strangers alighted from it and were greeted by everyone who was standing there and ushered inside and told to take a seat at the large communal table where everyone ate.

As all the bedrooms were in use, they were told they would have to double up. Lisa was told to swap rooms with Bobbie as his room was much larger and it had bunk beds in it a well as the large single bed and Rosemary could move in with her and Poh and the two of them could have the bunk beds and that would free up two of the rooms and the two new men could have them. This meant that there were seven people in the main house and eight outside in four separate cottages.

After the new comers had been shown around the village and what they had accomplished there and the farming section and the security fencing that they had erected and were continuously strengthening they had their monthly meeting with all present. Several things came up for discussion and voted on and notes made to carry the suggestions out.

One of the suggestions was that that Joseph Epton was asked if he would take in hand the schooling of the younger members of their group at least three mornings a week, much to the disgust of the two young girls. Also one of the latest additions to their group Brian Brooks was asked if he would build bunk beds to be put in the rooms currently occupied by Joseph, Jason, Don and himself and they would obtain mattresses on one of their next trips, it was decided that they would leave Bobbies room with just his bed in it as with him running the farm he was up at odd hours, sometimes very early and it would be unfair to ask anyone to bunk in with him. Bobbie smiled at that and said he was delighted to go along with that arrangement.

After everything seemed to be discussed and the meting was just about to be broken up, Don Whiteside asked if he could speak. He was given the floor.

"There is one other matter that I feel I have to mention, on our way here to this section of civilisation we did encounter one other community, we are not sure how many people were in it but it appeared to be at least half a dozen, They are based just outside Cambridge and to the north of the town. When we stopped there we saw one girl no more than eighteen or nineteen and three men all in their late twenties and heard another female voice coming from a house and she was crying. The girl we saw did not look very happy and could have done with cleaning herself up a bit.

The main reason we declined was that a couple of the men were taking an unhealthy interest in Poh, asking what her age was and who did she belong to. Anyway we declined to stop saying that we wanted to explore a bit further and if we did not find anything that took our fancy we would be back. The bottom line was we did not trust the look of them and their parting shot to us as we left was that we were to stay out of Cambridge as that was their territory and we were not even to stop there for any supplies and up to a twenty mile radius from there."

"That does not sound to good, it sounds like they have set up for themselves a fiefdom and make what use of the women that they want." Chimed in Rusty.

"Unfortunately I do not think we are strong enough yet to do anything about them but we should keep them in mind for the future, but it does highlight that we could do with some stronger firepower and we are really going to have to strengthen up our fencing perimeter a lot more as it is not strong enough to keep out determined men if they want to raid us or take us over sometime in the future. Also it is now by our reckoning to be the 17th. of September and it wont be long before winter is upon us and we are going to have to put an extra effort into gathering in supplies for the winter not only for us but for the livestock as well and that also means winter clothing and shoes or boots. Actually the mind boggles at the thought of what we are going to have to do to prepare." said John. The next couple of hours were taken up with making out lists of supplies that everyone thought they might need working on the assumption of a harsh winter with heavy snow.

The next day they all returned to the main house and took up the discussion where it had left off the previous night. One of the first things decided upon was that they would send out four parties of two people and leave Rusty back at the village to look after it and everyone else left behind. It was thought that Jason and Brian would go out as one party and their areas of expertise meant that they would take the truck and go after hardware items and farming goods that they thought they would need and the other three parties would each be given a list that they were to specialise in.

Each day for at least a week they would endeavour to get one trip done each and get back with the goods and unload and then they could help unload and store everything as it came in to the village and get ready for the next days trip, also everyone was to be asked to look out for petrol jerry cans and bring as many back with them full each trip. Those left behind in the village would while everyone was away make out a complete list of everything they had and divide it in to categories. The four vehicles drove out at ten am the first morning and split up and went their different ways and all were heavily armed.

John and Anne were looking for food as their first priority. By now they knew what villages they had already stripped and did not have to waste any time in going to places that they had already been to.

They made straight for Holt and went to the first supermarket that they had previously been to because they knew it was not near stripped. And when the Range Rover was full to bursting John decide to go and get a new truck from a garage showroom and they started to fill it to. They also found a dozen jerry cans in a garage and filled them with ten gallons each. By four in the afternoon they had filled every space they could and headed back home. When they arrived they found that they were the last to return for the day so everyone was able to get stuck in and help unload their vehicles. A separate dump had been established at the far end of the village for the petrol cans and when everything else was unloaded their dozen cans were driven down to the dump and added to the growing stockpile.

That evening everyone in the community gave a hand in putting away all the goods brought back that day and adding them to the inventory that had already been drawn up. Their store room in the main house was long ago filled up to capacity and a new store room had been established next door in a large shed that had obviously been used for some time as a garage going by the oil stains on the floor. It was swept up and completely cleaned out and Jason and Brian were already hard at work making shelving to hold all the goods that were waiting to be packed away on them when finished. It was decided that when Jason and Brian left the next morning they would take the new truck with them along with their Range Rover and fill it with animal fodder for the farm animals and the horses. And everyone else would just keep on with their lists and not to worry about getting too much of any one item as it would eventually be used up.

The next morning they left at eight am and set off on their quests and left the stay at home party putting the remainder of yester-days stock away and continuing with their inventory. This pattern was kept up all week and four more storage sheds had been found and cleaned out and shelving installed.

The two on the hardware detail had found a business selling sheds in kit form and had brought back four fairly large shed kits that they had offloaded at the farm area and would do for storage of hay and shelters for the animals if the weather was too bad and they needed good shelter and they had also brought back bags of cement and had also managed to load on to the back of the truck a small JCB Bob Cat that they again could use for a lot of heavy jobs and it ran on petrol and not diesel because that would have complicated things in having to accumulate and store another type of fuel.

The following week it was decided that they would continue with the salvaging but John and Rusty would go in search of an Army or Territorial base and see what they could come up with in the way of arms. So on Monday morning they all set out again, possibly some were not as enthusiastic as they were at the beginning of the exercise but it still had to be done.

Rusty suggested that they make their way to Kings Lynn first as he knew their was an Territorial Army base there and see what it gave up and then if necessary they could move on to Wattisham in Suffock or RAF base at Marham.

They arrived at Kings Lynn and soon found the T. A. base, after breaking their way in through the main gate and driving around they found the armoury but it was locked up solid. They made their way over to the headquarters building and rusty went looking for some keys. He reckoned they would not be too hard to find, they were probably in the Sgt. Majors office. After rummaging around for half an hour he came out with several bundles of keys and they returned back to the armoury.

They tried the first and second bundles of keys that looked suitable, but they were no good but on the third bundle they struck pay dirt and a key opened the heavy padlock and another key opened the two other locks on the door. They swung open the heavy door and found a steel grate blocking their way, again a key on that same bundle opened the locks on the gate.

They went inside and found everything that they wanted from automatic weapons such as the old Sterling sub machine guns to more modern machine pistols and heavy machine guns on tripods and boxes of grenades and even hand held rocket launchers. They carried outside and loaded everything they wanted into the back of the double axel truck along with boxes and boxes of ammunition, they also found automatic rifles and shotguns and small arms and flame throwers as well. When they had finished loading enough weapons and ammunition to start a small war they locked up the armoury again and left the base and took the keys with them. Before they left the base they hitched a trailer on to the back of the truck and filled it with dozens of jerry cans that they found in a stockpile along with petrol bladders which were too big for them to handle, they filled up the jerry cans with petrol and set of back to the village.

They arrived back to the village at three pm and unloaded the weapons and petrol and had everything put away until they could call a meeting and decide what way they were going to disperse the weapons around the village. Rusty said he could set up fields of fire that would give them the best fields of fire in the event of a battle ever taking place.

The next morning some of the weapons were issued to the men and it was decided where to place the heavy machine guns at the different places around the village perimeter and also some in the village itself hidden in a couple of the cottages.

When October rolled in the weather was decidedly colder and in it was decided that they would do one more week of foraging before winter set in. Because the supplies closest to their village had started to become scarcer it was decided that they would make their next forage in to Kings Lynn which they had hardly touched as yet.

They would send out the same four teams as the last time but with one difference they would take eight vehicles including the two trucks but they would stay in groups of two The next morning after the meeting they set off in convoy for Kings Lynn. They had an uneventful trip except for the occasional packs of wild dogs which were discouraged from coming to close or following them by shooting a couple of them. On arrival in Kings Lynn they split up into their groups of two vehicles and went after their separate lists of supplies.

Jason and Brian as usual were assigned to their hardware stores and farmers supply store. They first went to the farmers supply store and filled the truck with everything from barbed wire, fencing posts, electric fence kits, feed for the horses and bales of hay until the truck was full to overflowing then they headed to the hardware stores and started filling the double axle truck with mundane things such as nails, screws, kerosene lamps, tools, timber of all sizes and everything that they thought that the village could make use of either now or in the future. By three pm in the afternoon they had managed to fill the second vehicle and decided to head to the rendezvous point to see if the others had arrived yet. On arrival they found four of the other vehicles waiting for them but Tom and Mary were still not back yet. They had been sent after clothing to fit all the people in the village and bedding, shoes, boots and towels. After waiting for thirty minutes they could hear the sound of the approaching vehicle and were surprised to see a strange Toyota Land Cruiser turn into the square. Everyone immediately ran to take cover behind their vehicles and to have their weapons ready.

The other vehicle on seeing them immediately stopped and sat for a minute then the drivers door opened and a girl in her middle twenties got out and held up both of her hands to let them see she was not holding a weapon and called out that they came in peace and meant no harm to anyone and when told by John to walk over to them she started to do so.

When she reached their position she smiled and said. "Well this is a turn up for the books, we certainly did not expect to find so many people in one place". As she was talking she was taking a good look at their truck loads of supplies that they had gathered up.

Anne spoke up. "Where are you from?"
"My name is Beth and my friend and myself are from Norwich, we left there about four weeks ago because of the risk to our health from all the bodies and decided to explore and see what was left of the country. Can I call over my companion, we thought it was better for me to approach you first?"

"Sure it is." replied John and everyone started to relax.

Their visitor turned round towards her vehicle and shouted out. "Its okay Mike they are okay." The passenger door of their transport opened and a man in his early thirties alighted from their vehicle and proceeded to walk over towards them, he carried a shotgun over the crook of his left arm and looked slightly apprehensive. Just as he reached them Tom and Mary appeared in their well laden Range Rover from behind the new arrivals vehicle and drove over to them.

"I see everyone is here." said Tom and smiled at the newcomers. Who may you two be?"

John answered for the two newcomers. "We had just started to introduce ourselves when you two arrived. This is Mike and this is Beth. I am John and my friends are Tom, Mary, Anne, Jason, Brian, Joseph and last but certainly not least this is Joanne. We have a settlement in the area and as you can see we were out getting the grocery list before winter arrives. What are your plans?"

"We have no hard and fast plans, other than we were getting ready to look for somewhere to stay for the winter and so far Beth has been the fussy one and not found anywhere to her liking." As he spoke Mike put his arm around Beth's shoulders and gave her a squeeze and smiled at her.

"We have a community of twelve or fifteen people and you are more that welcome to join us or if you want to spend the night with us we will send you off in the morning with a full tank of petrol and any supplies that you require." Replied john.

"Thanks we would be delighted to take you up on your kind offer."

"Fine if everyone is ready we will head home and if you would just care to follow us."

They set off back to the village again in convoy only this time there was one more vehicle going back than there was when they left.

They arrived back at five pm and once again Bobbie was waiting for them at the gate to let them in only this time he had young Poh keeping him company. Jason and Brian turned off to off load their truck at he farm sheds after leaving their other vehicle at the front of the main house. Along with everyone else's vehicles.

Introductions were made to the newcomers and they started unloading the vehicles with Mary giving the instructions where she wanted what put. By dark they had not had time to off load all that they had brought back with them and had to call a halt until the morning. The women went inside to start making a meal for everyone.

After they had eaten the two newcomers were allocated a cottage to move into as they had only one room at the main house that was empty and it was a bit small for two people and everyone decided to have an early night as they were all tired from their days exertions.

The next morning everyone seemed to getup early and they were plying the newcomers with questions about where they had been and who had they seen and what ever information that they could get.

The two newcomers appeared to answer every question frankly and were observed taking in everything there was to see.

"Would you like to see around the place and what we have done with it?" Asked John. "If so I am sure Joseph would be delighted to show you both around the place."

The two newcomers said they would love to see around the village and immediately Joseph told them to come on there was no time like the present.

After the trio had set off on their sightseeing trip everyone else set about finishing the unloading of the balance of the supplies from the vehicles. By this time the sheer quantity of the supplies they had gathered up had forced them to convert one of the houses into a pure storage area for food and had emptied two of the garages that they had stocked and transferred everything over to the house. They had still to put up more shelving in it. As for all the hardware they had made use of the largest shed and had converted it literally into a hardware store. Every time someone took anything out of the storage rooms no matter what it was they had to mark it off the list that was left at the entrance. They also had a list in the main house that if the last of anything was used or there was something was required that was put on this list for the next foraging trip. Joseph and his two companions arrived back at lunch time from their trip around the village and expressed how surprised they were at how well organised they were.

After lunch of tinned potatoes, carrots, peas and tinned ham and soft drinks John asked the two of them if they would like to join their community.

Mike glanced at Beth and she nodded at him and he replied for them both saying they would love to join their group. Everyone seemed delighted with the two new additions. It was explained to them that as they were a couple they could keep the house they had spent the night in or hunt around the village for another one more to their liking as the main house was more of a gathering point and headquarters and a billet for those that were single or unattached. Any supplies they had in their vehicle they could keep and also they could draw from the communal stores for anything else that they required and store in their own larder for making a meal anytime they wanted a meal on their own. They said they would keep the house they were shown to last night and thanked everyone for their kindness.

After lunch all the vehicles were finished being unloaded and everything was packed away and it was decide to head out again to Kings Lynn for another load. They set off again in convoy but left the two newcomers to settle in a bit more before putting them to work and anyway they wanted to clean out the house they had taken over and get a fire going and make it a bit more comfortable and transport over some supplies from the store rooms to their larder.

They made a quick trip to kings Lynn and everyone decided to go to the supermarket and load up with nothing but food this trip.

After a couple of hours it had just turned five o clock and the winters evening had set in and it had become quite dark when they finished up and made for home. The trip home was only marred by one of the vehicles getting a puncture and they had to change the wheel and keep a look out for dog packs that they could hear in the surrounding darkness and occasionally see the glint of an eye as they circled the convoy and tried to gather up enough courage to attack. Eventually they managed to change the wheel without anything untold happening and got back on their way to the village and were glad to see Bobbie waiting for them at the gate. They parked outside the house and went inside without unloading the vehicles having decided to leave that particular chore for the next day.

The first thing in the morning they fixed the puncture and unloaded all the supplies and found that the newcomer Mike had been busy while they were away building shelving units for the store house and he had roped in the two youngest girls Poh and Lisa to help him by fetching and carrying and the girls were delighted to be of help. And his partner Beth had been busy in their new house cleaning and making it habitable for them.

The next day they decide to make it a day of wood cutting, so six of the men climbed into the back of the truck with chain saws and hand saws and set off for the nearest woods and got stuck in. They cut trees and sawed logs all day. At lunchtime Bobbie came out in his vehicle and brought flasks of coffee and soft drinks along with sandwiches that Mary had made after she had finished baking bread. It was enough to keep them going and it meant that they did not waste time having to return for lunch. By three pm they managed to fill the truck completely and made their way back to the village without incident.

They decided to offload logs at the five privately owned cottages first and have them stocked up and that the next day they would go out again and that truck full they cut would all go to the main house.

The next morning they returned to where they had been cutting down the trees and started in again. They finished up that night and unloaded everything at the main house, had tea and collapsed into bed. For the next two days they did the same again and left another load at the main house and the last day divide the logs into six lots, one each for the five occupied houses and another load at another house that was as yet unoccupied but thought it was a good idea to be prepared for the next couple that may want to move out of the main house and into their own accommodation.

The next day they decided that it was a good idea not to do any heavy work but just tidy up any odd jobs that needed to be done and let their sore muscles recover from the hard work of cutting logs that none of them were used to.

The following day was a Saturday and they had a village meeting after breakfast. John took the chair as chairman for the meeting and said that up to now he was the one who seemed to be making all the main decisions but really no one had elected him to do that and he thought that it was about time a village headman was properly elected to this position. At this statement a general hubbub broke out with everyone trying to say something all at the same time. When things had been brought to order it was decided that John should remain in the position of headman as no one was dissatisfied with the way he was running things. With that out of the way he asked was there anything else that anyone wanted to bring up for discussion. At this prompting Brian Brooks asked would it be possible for him and Joanne to move out of the main house into one of the cottages. A few cheers went up at this request and one voice was heard to ask was anyone surprised at the request and everyone laughed much to the embarrassment of the couple.

"There is just one thing that I think has to be brought up and made as a mandatory rule. Everyone I notice has become a bit complacent lately and a good fifty percent of you are not carrying your weapons around with you. I must insist that everyone at all times carries their pistol and knife even inside the house and when you go outside you must also have your rifle or shotgun with you."

This statement caused a bit of a commotion with everyone trying to have their say at the one time and most of those wanting to say something were objecting.

"I am not going to apologise for this rule, it may save either your life or someone else's life. Forgetting about the dog packs and other possible wild animals there are people out there who would kill or hurt you without any compunction at all. This is not a world now where all the bad people are dead and there is only good ones left, if this is what you think you are thinking you are in for a rude awakening. Most of you are aware of what happened to Anne, if it was not for Max she may not be here today, and you know the story that Don and Brian told us when they arrived about the group they came across in Cambridge. Why do you all think we have been fortifying this place and collecting the weapons that we have."

There was a discussion held about the matter but it was more subdued after John's tirade back at them and eventually they took a vote and everyone agreed to exercise a policy from now on for everyone to go armed at all times including the children who would be given knives and a small calibre hand gun and taught immediately how to use them safely.

The next two days were spent doing the chore that everyone loved most, cutting more firewood. Again the firewood was spread amongst the main house and the six occupied houses and again they built up a stock at one of the empty cottages. With time fast running out before the first winter snow arrived they decide to string barbed wire outside their main fence line as an extra deterrent also they had found some rolls of razor wire when they went to the Army base at Kings Lynn and had brought them home with them as well as the armaments. After a week they had managed to complete the job and were feeling fairly secure in their village compound.

Bobbie, Rosemary and Joanne reckoned they had more than enough food for all the livestock to last them through the winter months. Joanne and Rosemary were now giving riding lessons on a regular basis to everyone that was interested and most of them were becoming quite proficient to varying degrees.

On the morning of the fifth of November it started to snow, it started as light flourishes that were not to heavy but there was still enough coming down to start making the ground white. The two girls who had made themselves responsible for the horses and Bobbie headed over to the farm to see to the animals and to make sure they had access to the sheds for shelter and enough food out for them and then returned to the house for a warm breakfast. They came into the house blowing on their fingers and stamping their boots and complaining how cold it was.

Nobody seemed to be to keen to go outside that day and everyone sat around the big fire in the main house drinking beer and swapping stories and the children and Rosemary were playing a board game that someone had brought back to the village for them. They all had a lazy day and watched the snowfall and instead of a formal lunch they each made sandwiches for them selves as and when they felt hungry.

The snow fell all day. It fell softly and continuously without any let up but no blizzards.

The children were outside all day making the usual snowman and playing in it. A few of the adults were just as mad, it was obviously a way of letting go and relaxing after the last nine months of horror and hardship they had all endured, absolutely no work got done that day. The evening was spent in the kitchen and lounge drinking beers and wine and playing board games of which they had an abundance stock laid in for this type of occasion which they reckoned there would be a lot of evenings like it in the coming winter.

CHAPTER 5

WINTER ARRIVES.

The next morning John woke up snug in his bed under the doona and with Anne snuggled into his side. She must have felt him move because she woke up and murmured. "My nose feels cold, is it still snowing?"

"Yes it appears to be, I can see snow falling through the side of the curtain where it is not fully over."

"What time is it?"
"Time we were thinking about getting up it is seven thirty."

"No way I am too comfy and warm under here." She murmured as she snuggled down further under the cover.

John suddenly without any warning threw the cover all the way back and jumped out of bed to escape her wrath as she lashed out and screamed at him and laughed at the same time.

He grabbed his clothes under his arm and dashed for the door to get dressed in the kitchen in front of the range stove that hopefully was still lit with Anne in hot pursuit.

"I vote we go to the main house for breakfast as Mary will have the ham and eggs on the pan and Bobbie will have brought the fresh milk in and we can have some of her country butter that she has started making on wedges of bread toasted in front of the fire."

"Fine with me." replied John as he struggled into his clothes hopping from one foot to the next trying unsuccessfully to keep from standing on the cold floor in his bare feet. When he was dressed and while waiting for Anne to get dressed he re-stoked the fire in the kitchen range and damped it down so it would keep lit for the rest of the day without any further attention as he knew he would not feel like having to start lighting it when they came home in the evening.

After making sure that everything was ship shape in the house they pulled on their boots and made their way over to the main house. They literally had to struggle through the snow because by now it was quite deep, it had obviously snowed all night. At least they did not have any deep drifts to contend with as there must not have been any wind to speak of and it had just come straight down.

They arrived at the main house and after removing their boots and putting them up on a rack to keep them dry they went inside in their stocking feet so as not to traipse snow all through the place as they knew they would soon get the sharp edge of Mary's tongue if they did that.

When they opened the door they were overwhelmed by the smell of freshly made bread and the smell of the open log fire in the lounge. They found that they were not the first to arrive as about half of the group were already there before them and were ensconced in front of the open lounge fire drinking either hot chocolate, coffee or the usual tea as long as it was wet and warm which seemed to be the order of the day.

Mary spotted them as they came through the front door and said as she looked up to see whom it was. "What someone else who does not know how to make their own breakfast." she said in a cross tone of voice but smiled to take the sting out of her words. She was at her happiest when cooking in the kitchen for everyone and joking with them and letting them know who ran the house and who was boss in it.

From the look of the two full buckets of milk on the draining board it was obvious that Bobbie had been up to look at the cattle and from the look of the rosy red cheeks of the two younger girls they had obviously been with him to give a hand. It was in a happy atmosphere that everyone sat down to breakfast. The only people missing were two of the couples that had not braved the snow this early and were having breakfast at home, Tom, Mary and Mike and Beth.

Rusty turned to Bobbie after breakfast an asked how the animals were faring after their first night of snow. He replied from what he had seen they looked good but other than to check if they were all alive he had just done the milking with the two girls and come back home after that, but he was heading back out to the farm after breakfast.

"Would you like some company?" he asked.

"Sure I would, you are welcome to come along I would enjoy the company." When Rusty and Bobbie went out to see the farm animals the two girls went along as well and Rosemary decide to go to so she could see how her precious horse was.

The other men decided to do a bit of snow shovelling around the front and back door of the main house and to make a path over to one of the garages they were still using as storage sheds and make sure that all the vehicles not garaged were protected to the best of their ability with blankets over the engines and car covers over the vehicles themselves. They also decided to move all the cars that were not garaged and the two trucks over in front of the house as there was a small car park across the road from it and they thought it would be better to keep them all together. They also thought it was a good idea to put snow chains on two of the Range Rovers in case they were required during the time there was snow on the ground.

Up at the farm they dug some snow from around the entrances to the sheds where the cattle had taken over for shelter and dug paths over to the feed shed and fed the horses whom had been kept inside because of what they thought the weather was going to do. They put waterproof warm coats on the horses and let them outside while they were there. The girls were asked to go and pick some cabbages that they would take back with them when they left. They also examined the fences around the animals' enclosure to make sure there were no drifts covering the fences and thus allow animals from outside to gain access. So far they were clear but they thought it was going to be a problem in the future if it continued to snow at its present rate, they were going to have to examine them every day. By lunchtime they reckoned they had done everything they could for the time being and headed back to the main house after gathering up the sackfuls of vegetables that the girls had picked for them.

The next day a bit of a wind had got up and the snow that had continued to fall lightly all night and was beginning to drift so the men got out the van which they had had the foresight to put snow chains on and filled it up with fencing paraphernalia that included sheets of marine ply that were eight feet tall. When they arrived at the farm fields where the livestock were they found a very distressed Bobbie. It seemed what they had been afraid of had happened and a pack of dogs had got in to the field where the cattle were during the night and had attacked and killed one of the young bullocks. Bobbie felt that it had not long happened as they had not had time to destroy the carcass, they had only managed to rip out its throat and had partially gnawed two of it's legs and had started to eat them, but the rest of the carcase was untouched. He said when he arrived the dogs, there were four of them led by a large shepherd saw him and scarpered back the way they had got in. Since then he had been busy checking up on the other animals but they were all fine, just a bit traumatised. He asked would they mind if he got on with milking and after that he would come over and give them a hand with the fencing. They said no he should just get on with his normal chores and leave the fencing to them. There were six of the men who had come out in the van and they had left Joseph and Mike back at the village to look after all the women.

They went over to the fence where they found the dogs had made their way in over a snow drift and over the top of their fencing. They decided that they would start at the corner of the field and clear the snow all along the complete fence line on that side of the field and build a new fence inside the existing fence line with the eight feet long marine plywood sheets as far along as what they had would stretch. They got the post hole digger into action as the ground was far too hard with the snow having frozen it for them to be able to use spades and shovels. Once a hole was dug they put in a post that was two feet into the ground but still left six feet above ground and used bags of quick drying cement, all they had to do was put the cement into the holes around the post and add water and that was it. They managed to have the holes all dug right along that side of the field and the posts in by two pm and cemented into place. Mary had sent them out lunch and hot drinks with the two girls and Bobbie.

After lunch they got stuck back into the job and soon had all the sheets of plywood they had, put up into place. Unfortunately this still left over half that fence still to do as they only had twelve sheet of ply available to them. They felt that with having cleaned up the fence line and dug back the snow that the existing fence would do the job until they could get some more of the marine ply sheets from Kings Lynn where they had obtained the original supply. As a last job for the day they managed to eventually load the carcase of the young bullock on to the back of the van and brought it back with them to the house to be butchered and put into their freezer, not that with the present weather a freezer was necessary but it would all pack away into a chest freezer that they had managed to get going with their limited supply of generated electricity and a night of steaks for everyone would be very nice for a change to their diet as meat had been in short supply.

It was decided that night that they would take the truck and try to get to Kings Lynn the following morning. They thought that with snow shovels and six men wielding them they should be able to make it through.

The next morning they all set off with the well wishes of the whole community who felt that it was a worthwhile risk as their livestock were too precious a commodity to them to risk losing any more of them to the dog packs. Also it was decided that Rusty as one of the best shots in the village should go up to the top of the church tower and take the sniper rifle with him and see if he could take out a few of the dogs that were continuously roaming along the perimeter of the village trying to find ways in.

Every so often for the rest of the day the sound of Rusty shooting dogs was to be heard every so often as he dispatched another one. By the end of the day he had definitely killed eleven dogs and he thought he had wounded another six or seven.

The party in the twin axle truck had only gone about a mile up the road when they had their first drift to dig away so that the four by four was able to get through. Actually the trip to kings Lynn was not too bad, they had to only stop about twelve times, because the Range Rover was able to handle the rest. They went straight to the hardware store and loaded up the truck with as much as they could carry plus more bags of instant cement and nails. They had decided to commandeer another Range Rover which should be able to get through driving behind the truck especially with snow chains on it or else if they hadn't four of the party were going to have a cold trip sitting on top of the supplies in the open and sliding all over the place as they negotiated the trip home. They managed to make their way home without any incident or stops to dig their way through and went straight to the field and unloaded their timber and fencing posts to have it there in place in the morning. Everyone was glad to see a hot meal and get off to their beds after their hard days work digging through snow drifts, before they went to bed it was decided that with the road open from their efforts they would go back to Kings Lynn the following morning and again load up as much of the remaining sheets of plywood and get it back to the village before the weather closed in again and made the trip impossible.

The next morning four of them went off in the truck and the new rover back to the shop to pick up the plywood and more cement and left two of their original party behind to start back into erecting the sheets they had brought back the previous day and they along with a couple of the other men left behind originally from the first trip to get stuck into the fencing.

The trip driving back to the shop was uneventful and had no stops even though it had snowed a little the previous night the vehicles with their chains were able to handle it. They got the rest of the remaining timber from that source quickly loaded up and then thought they would try the other couple of smaller hardware shops that they had noticed in the town to see if they had any of the same marine ply in stock. They found in the first shop they had a dozen sheets which they took and the second shop only had five sheets that they also took and that cleaned out the town of all that they had, they would have too look elsewhere if the required any more. The trip home was again uneventful and they offloaded the timber at the farm where they had been erecting the panels and found that those they had left behind had erected all they had left them to work with and had started and nearly finished one other sides of the field that was an outside fence line, as they were unloading the supples the others returned and said there was not that much to do as the fence posts were all in place they may as well finish the job now before dark, so they all got stuck in and finished the job of fencing the outside fence line for that field. It was decided that what panels that were left they would start the next day to do the same to the outside fence for the next field that was adjacent to the one they had just finished. The next day they all got stuck into the job and had just enough panels to finish that particular fence line with two panels left over.

Over the next few days they carefully examined the outside fence line completely around the village and strengthened it in several places and put up the two remaining panels where they thought they would do the most good. Unfortunately what they had done was going to have to do them until after the snow was gone, then they could look for more of the panels and finish fencing in the complete village behind the eight foot panels which would make everyone feel a lot more secure in regards to any wild animals getting access to the village. Someone mentioned that after the winter snow was gone they might find what they required from one of the council yards as they had noticed that the main roads were using that particular form of panelling along side the motorways as a means of cutting back on road noise.

Over the next few weeks they managed to work on all those small chores that were annoying but had to be done when someone mentioned that it would soon be Christmas, actually in six days time.

This put everyone in a flurry to have some decorations put up and try and arrange something for the children as it was going to be especially sad for them it would be their first Christmas without their parents and siblings. It was decided it was worth the risk of the journey into Holt that was only a few miles away to see if they could pick up some decorations and toys for the girls and what else they could get for everyone else as presents. At last it was Christmas Eve and the children were encouraged to put up their stocking over the fireplace in the main house to see what Santa Clause would bring them. The next morning there was great excitement and everyone was out of bed at the crack of dawn and down to the main lounge and found that Mary Sward had beat them all to it and had a lovely warm log fire already burning in the hearth, that along with the fir tree they had found and erected and decorated and all the gaily wrapped presents under the tree and the two full stockings for the girls and also one for Rosemary who tried to look superior and grown up and did not need a Christmas stocking even though she was the first into it and beat the two younger girls. All the presents were opened and Christmas carols were playing on a CD player they had hooked up and everyone were drinking eggnog even before breakfast which was soon underway and was dished up with everyone present at the large table, the rest of the day was spent with everyone declaring how delighted they were with their presents and that they had not expected anything and the children were delighted with their gifts which included dolls that they insisted they were too old to play with but were to be seen for the rest of the day hugging them.

The Christmas holidays soon passed and the New Year came and went just as quickly. The snow continued to fall and melt and fall and melt again but by the beginning of February it finally looked as if the snow was letting up at last and the weather started to improve.

CHAPTER 6

THE START OF THEIR FIRST SPRING.

A meeting was called after the snow finally vanished in the second week in February and again everyone presented their lists of requirement that were needed. One of the things that Bobbie brought up was that he thought it would be a good idea if anyone who saw packets of seeds for vegetable s should bring them back and no limit to be put on them because as the seeds got older the quality would start to deteriorate and they would have to soon start gathering their own seeds, this was thought to be a good idea and also they wanted to start looking for more of that Marine plywood if it could be obtained as it did such a good job for fencing. After discussions lasting a couple of hours their lists were all compiled and allocated to different teams that were going out starting the next day. The collection crews were made up of Tom Fielding and Mary Harrington, John Mcgrath and Anne Knoble, Mike Thornton and Beth and Brian Brooks and Jason Tonner in the Rang Rover truck and they were to specifically look for a new source of the Marine ply and fence posts and bags of quick drying cement all the others were after the usual supplies ranging from petrol to food and all the other bits and pieces that they wanted to help make their life as comfortable as possible now and in the future as supplies started to run out. John and Anne decided that they would make their way to Norwich as it was a fair sized town of approximately four hundred thousand people and they had never tried it before. It was also decided that they would not stay away more than three days before someone would come looking for who ever had not kept to that timetable.

The men that were left behind decided to go to the mill and have another look at their generating plant and see in what way they could improve it and what equipment they would need if they wanted to supply the entire village with electricity and also what required to be done to make the mill operate as a mill again and possibly going over to a mill that had still been in operation before the death in one of the other villages because it had been renovated and was operating as a proper business supplying flour for the surrounding areas and the tourists.

By the end of the first day the first vehicle returned with Tom and Mary and they had a vehicle full of reels of electrical wiring and electrical equipment and accessories you would need if they started laying cables around the village and also they had managed to get another twelve jerry cans of petrol lashed to their roof. On the second day Mike and Beth returned with a vehicle full of pharmaceuticals and tins of food and a huge supply of seeds and also a book that explained how to harvest your own seeds and that afternoon Brian and Jason arrived back with their truck full of the all important sheets of plywood and fencing posts and bags of the quick drying cement and the good news also that they had found a source of the sheets of timber that they reckoned would be more than enough to encircle the village three times over in the Holt Council yards. That just left John and Anne to return and they really were not expected back until the third day as their destination was the furthest away in Colchester.

John and Anne made their way directly to Norwich and just made notes of anything that they thought may be of interest to the village and needed to be explored some other day when they had more time. They arrived in Norwich at three in the afternoon and noticed a decided deterioration of the roads due to their lack of upkeep and the recent winters weather effect on them.

Also they noticed that nearly all the bodies were gone, those that were left appeared to have little or no flesh on them and very few of the corpses were complete which they reckoned was because of the dog packs tearing them apart and carrying parts of the bodies off with them. They had a look for a hotel to stay in and found one. The Holiday Inn and it was fairly well in the centre of the town and would be handy to use it for a base of operations. They drove around a bit and had a good look at the town and what it had to offer and also examined a couple of the supermarkets to see had anyone started looting them for supplies, one of them was untouched from what they could see but the other had the look of being raided a few times although there was no significant depletion of the supplies.

They decide to do their usual three shots and wait five minutes and keep repeating that for an hour to see what reaction they got. After thirty minutes had elapsed a vehicle appeared at the end of the street and slowly approached them and stopped about twenty feet away. A man who appeared to be in his early thirties got out along with another man in his twenties and both were carrying guns and started to walk over to John and Anne. They also noticed what appeared to be a woman still left in the car. John laid his rifle down on the ground as did Anne and they slowly stood up from where they had been sitting on the kerb.

"How are you folks, we were hoping that we would attract some ones attention. "said John as a way of starting the dialogue.

"We thought that might be your intention'" replied the older man "My name is Peter Woods and this is Hal Stern and our lady friend still in the car is Jean Thackery."

"I am John McGrath and my friend is Anne Knoble and we come from a small village to the north west of here where we have started a small community of about seventeen people of various ages from a couple of children to adults, men and women."

The guy Peter replied. "It is nice to know that there are other people alive and not just ourselves, what are you doing here in Norwich?"

Well this is one of our first expeditions outside our village after the winter snow and we sent out several groups to forage for supplies look for future sources of supplies and to see if we can contact any more people that might want to join us for the security that a group will give and the fact that we are fairly well organised although that continues to improve every day that passes. How many are in your group?"

"There is just the three of us in our group that survived the sickness but there is another group living in the town but they are too militant for our liking and everything is done as one man says and no argument about it, there are I believe seven in that group although up to now they have a policy of live and let live, we just had reservations about joining them."

"You are more than welcome to join our village, we discuss everything as a group and then decide on a course of action, I was elected as head man by a vote, if anyone else wants the title they are more than welcome to it, if anyone joins us and does not like it they are entitled to a vehicle and supplies for two weeks and weapons to protect themselves and may go with our blessing, At the present we mostly all drive Range Rovers for ease of keeping spare parts and servicing them rather than have to keep spares for a dozen different vehicles. One of our other rules is that when a vehicle is out on a trip it must always return fully loaded with supplies, be it food or what ever. We had decided to spend the next couple of nights at the Holiday Inn and survey the town during the day before we return after two nights, perhaps the three of you might like to go away and have a discussion and let us know if you would like to join us."

For the first time the two men seemed to relax and smiled and called out to the woman in their car to come out to join them.

The woman Jean Thackery alighted from the car and walked over to join them, she appeared to be in her twenties and when she saw her two companions smiling she did also. "Hello I am Jean Thackery and this is my man Peter and our friend Hal, I am pleased to meet you."

They all stood for a few more minutes each taking time to explain more about themselves, and Peter explained about the invitation to join the other group if they wanted and they could leave any time if it was not to their liking. They decided on the spot to join John and Anne and motor back with them. They said that they would join them the next day at the Holiday Inn after lunch and then said their goodbyes and left.

"It looks like we may have just added to our group by another three people." Said John to Anne. I vote we start stocking up with supplies from our list for the rest of the day.." Anne smiled and agreed and they looked at the list to see what was first on the list.

They made their way to the Range Rover Garage and obtained another vehicle and again took a dual axle utility / truck. They filled the truck up with again as many jerry cans as they could find and then went along to a local nursery and cleaned it out off all the vegetable seed that they could find and then on to the usual hardware and again took everything that they thought may be useful to them. They found a large engineering works and found a large dynamo that they thought might be of use for the mill for generating electricity but it was to heavy for the two of them to lift so decided that they would come back the next day with the other three people they were sure they could get it aboard the utility, and also filled up on food items until both their vehicle were crammed to bursting point.

The next day the other three people turned up in of all things, three Range Rovers, two of them were packed with supplies from where ever they obviously been living and one empty as yet

They welcomed the newcomers and explained about the dynamo and asked would they gave a hand in getting it loaded on to the truck and then they would use the empty vehicle to stock up with more food items. They made their way to the engineering works and with a lot of effort and the use of a pulley system managed to get it loaded aboard and decided to take the pulley system with them as it might prove useful. After stocking up the empty vehicle the set off on their way back home. Once again when they arrived at the gate they found Bobbie waiting for them with his usual big grin lighting up his face. He waved and smiled at the three new comers and shouted to them welcome.

They all drove through the security gate at the bridge and stopped at the main house, when everyone alighted from their vehicles John pointed at a cottage just down the street from the main house and said to Peter and Jean. "Because you and Jean are a couple you may have that cottage, you will find that the wood shed at the rear is fully stocked so you will be able to get heating in the cook stove and the fireplace, if you require any groceries or any other items you ask Mary who is in charge of issuing stores and she will give you whatever you require, all you have to do when withdrawing stores is to update the list of stores in that room to take into account what you have removed, the list hangs at each room door. The items that you packed into your vehicle that you brought from your last residence be they food or whatever you keep and unpack is yours. Any items that we salvaged you unload them at the central stores that someone will show you and any items that you require you can withdraw from the stores at anytime either now or later, which ever suits you. Hal because you are unattached you will stay in the main house until you find yourself a partner and then may wish to move into a private residence, that again is up to you. All of you may eat at the main house either part of the time or all of the time, again that is your decision. Most of us seem to eat at the main house most of the time, probably for the company or more likely it is because Mary is such a good cook. One of our rules that we do enforce at all times is that you go around fully armed at all times carrying a knife, handgun and either a rifle or shotgun and that applies to everyone in the village even within our own security fencing. Peter you and Jean may want to move into your residence before you do anything else, Hal if you come with me I will take you inside and have you shown you to your room, if you want to unpack any of your stuff from the vehicle we can give you a hand to carry it inside."

"Thanks John, everything I possess is in these two rucksacks." Replied Hal as he indicated the two items he had at his feet after he had unloaded them from the back of the vehicle.

"Right lets go inside, by the way Peter your own vehicles you can either park at your residence or across the road in the communal car park in front of the main house, right lets go inside those that are coming." John, Anne and Hal went inside and Bobbie shouted out to John. "I will give them a hand to unload their vehicle and show them the store house and the other store rooms and then bring them over to the main house.

When John and his two companions went inside they were greeted by Mary and Rusty. The two girls looked up shyly from where they were sitting in front of the fire place playing with a couple of toys they had received over Christmas.

"I see John has brought home a few more strays, if he keeps this up I think we will have to start calling him the shepherd." Said Rusty as he greeted the newcomer with a friendly smile and an outstretched hand.

Mary also came forward and smiled at Hal and shook his hand.

"If you want to unpack your gear and then come back downstairs I will have a hot drink ready for you and a snack to keep you going until dinner tonight."

While Hal made his way upstairs accompanied by young Lisa to show him the way Rusty turned and greeted John and Anne warmly, and Mary went back into the kitchen.

"It is good to see you home safe and sound, I take it that you did not have many problems. Come into the lounge the two of you and have a beer."

When the three of them were seated and each had a drink in their hands, Rusty asked did they know what skills the newcomers had brought with them.

"Actually we do, Hal whom you have just met was it seems a third year medical student at Cambridge and was home visiting his parents when the Death struck him down so he will be a very useful addition to our community and he and Beth should be able to make a very good team between them considering that she is a qualified pharmacist, Peter whom you have not met yet is a qualified engineer and his partner worked I believe in a bakery in her home town of

Norwich, so they should all be useful in their own way and I must say all three of them seem very open and friendly."

Anne agreed with his assessment and said. "I suppose we should go and unload the vehicles before it gets to dark to see what we are doing, as she drank off the remainder of her beer and got to her feet closely followed by John.

"I will come and give you a hand." Said Rusty as he joined them as they made their way to the front door.

When the got outside they decided to first of all to all unload their petrol supplies they had brought back and that they kept at the dump at the far end of the village away from where everyone lived. After unloading the cans that they had they then made their way to where they kept all the hardware goods stored and unloaded what they had of those items and then made their way to one of the storage garages and unloaded all the food items. That only left the seeds that they had brought back and they were unloaded in a dry shed next to the hardware supplies.

"I had not realised that we had found so many packets of seeds or onion bulbs." Remarked Anne as she surveyed what they had brought back with what was already there in what Rusty called the seed room."

They looked up at the sound of a vehicle and saw Bobbie along with his two charges stopping outside the storage garage they had just been to and saw them preparing to start unloading their two vehicles.

They went across the road and Rusty shouted out. Can we give you a hand to unload, many hands make light work? Peter looked up at the sound of the voice and smiled.

"Hi my name is Peter and this is my partner Jean."

"Hi my name is Rusty it is good to see you, I am sure you will both like it here in our community, let's give you a hand, it is not every ones favourite chore as it always seems to take for ever between unloading which is the easy part and packing away into the correct place which is what takes the time and then updating the relevant lists."

They got stuck in and between them all they soon had everything unpacked and put away in no time whatsoever and then went on to the drop off points to unload the other relevant goods they had and to get them packed away also. By the time they had finished it was getting dark so they made their way back to the main house after Peter and Jean dropped off their vehicle at their cottage.

When they went inside they found that nearly everyone was either in the lounge or dining room or in the kitchen helping Mary preparing the meal, the three newcomers were introduced all round they were asked what they liked to drink and then handed a drink and everyone started talking at once asking question about how they had survived and where they were from and dozens of other questions until John who had to shout to make himself heard above the general noise.

"Come on everyone give them a break, do you want them to up and run on their first night because of the pressure you are putting on them, all your questions will eventually be answered but in the meantime I am sure you would all like to extend to them our best wishes for the future and to welcome them to our community even if it is a nosey one? There was an embarrassed laugh at John's remarks and conversation got to a more manageable level as everyone relaxed. Because of the size of the gathering which had now grown to twenty people living in the village, tea had to be eaten with some sitting at the table in the kitchen, some in the lounge and eating off a plate on their laps and some in the dining room.

John remarked to Brian that perhaps the next day he and Jason and a couple of the others could see if they could make a larger table for the dining room which was larger than the kitchen and make a table or tables that would accommodate them all when eating. Also see if they could scrounge up a few more chairs both dining room chairs but also lounge chairs for the lounge from some of the other unoccupied cottages.

Brian said he knew exactly what to do and he had a knowing look on his face.

When queried he said. "Just wait and see."

Everyone decide by mutual consent to have an early night as everyone was tired from their days work and the ones that had just arrived from their journey and the excitement of their new home.

Before Peter and Jean left to go to their cottage Mary gave them some fresh eggs, milk, butter and sliced ham to take with them in case they wanted to eat on their own in the morning rather than at the main house. "Any other groceries that you want we will put together for you in the morning." she told them with her usual big friendly smile. She wished them good night.

Jean was overcome with emotion and put her arms around Mary and gave her a big hug as she thanked her in between the tears and then ran out of the house. Peter was embarrassed and said that was a lovely meal she had just fed them and the eggs, milk and butter were the first they had seen in a year since the Death and then he went after Jean.

The next morning at about eight o clock when John and Anne had managed to drag themselves out from under the warm doona and got dressed and stoked the fire and banked it they decided to go over to the main house for breakfast.

They went into the kitchen and found to their surprise that all the furniture had been changed overnight. There were two beautiful large mahogany tables in the dining room and plenty of chairs around them to match and extra ones stacked in a corner and when they looked into the lounge they saw that about eight or nine other large comfortable chairs had appeared there as well John was lost for words and looked around for Brian for an explanation.

He was standing in the kitchen with a large mug of coffee in one hand and a heaped plate of ham and eggs in the other and a smile on his face that stretched right across from one side to the other.

"How did you manage that."

"When you said last night about our problem I remembered the restaurant come bar just outside the village The Honey Bell. So this morning early we went over to it and collected what we wanted and had it all arranged as a surprise just as Mary appeared to start making the breakfast."

"I had forgotten all about that place, of course what a brilliant idea. Thank you so much and also your companions and for getting up so early to make it happen, it certainly is a great surprise.

"It was our pleasure." Came back the reply from Brian and his two companions Jason and Mike,
John and Anne made their way into the kitchen to hungrily grab two of the piled up plates of food for their breakfast and of course the usual mugs of ground coffee. Throughout the next hour a few more people straggled into the kitchen looking to be fed and were pleasantly surprised at the changes wrought by Brian and his two friends. Then the door opened and Jean and Peter came inside and came over to join them at the table along with Hal who had sat down beside them a little earlier and was just finishing his breakfast, he pushed the empty plate away from himself and across the table and murmured with a satisfied sigh. "I have just gone to heaven."

Mary was passing by and heard the remark and it put a smile on her face.

John called out to Poh who came running over to his table in response. "Are you doing anything important?"

"No John," came back the reply. "What do you want me to do?"

Would you like to take the three newcomers over to the farm and have Bobbie show them around and when he is finished there and ask him would he mind showing them around the village and all the store rooms and what ever there is to see."

"Can I take Lisa with me and Rosemary?"

"Of course you can."

John decided that he better call an emergency meeting for the village before he got bogged down with other work to discuss the confrontation that occurred in Norwich with another group that were living there. He related to everyone what had transpired there and the other group's dangerous attitude. After a lot of input from everyone it was decided that it would be wise to stay away from Norwich in the future and not to go within a twenty mile radius of the town and to monitor the situation as time went by.

"Brian I believe you have found a large supply of those eight foot panels, did you manage to get any over here yet?"

"Just about a dozen that we had found elsewhere before we found the main supply."

"Would you feel up to getting some help and taking a couple of the trucks out to load up with as many as you can and what ever else you think you would need, as I think we should make it a priority to finish securing the village perimeter before we are much older."

"Sure no problem, I will see what we can do."

"Thanks, Can I borrow some male bodies to help me unload a dynamo that we brought back and unload it over at the mill house." John asked the room in general as he headed over to the front door.

John headed over to his truck and just caught Brian before he left and shouted out to him to stop. "Sorry Brian I want to have this brought over to the mill as he indicates the large dynamo."

"I was wondering what I was going to do with that before we headed out."

Brian drove his truck over to the Mill and John and the other volunteers helped to unload the dynamo or electrical generator to give it its more up to date name and then he went off on his mission with the other truck.

"Thanks guys " said John after it had been unloaded and manhandled inside the mill which would keep it dry and hopefully rust free until they could figure out how to attach it to the existing turbine they had already in operation, limited though it may be. While John and a couple of the men who had helped him to unload the generator and bring it inside were standing and discussing it the door of the mill opened and in walked the three newcomers and Bobbie.

Bobbie said the three girls are away back with the milk and eggs to the main house.

Peter walked over to where they were standing and looked down at the dynamo.

"I see now why you wanted this heavy, awkward lump of machinery brought back here."

"Do you know anything about generating electricity." Asked John "Because we don't."

" A bit and I can tell you that your turbine from what I could see is too small for that generator and it is not big enough either if you want to supply the village, but we can certainly rig it up to produce some of what you want."

"Anything would be a help even if we can give everyone enough power to work a fridge or freezer and maybe one light."

"If we keep the wattage of the lights low we just may be able to do that but if it was me I would keep my eye open for a larger turbine and generator to match and supplement with solar panels on your roofs which will help a little and store your energy generated into batteries as well as a back up."

"May we ask you to work on this for us and see what you can come up with, Don Whiteside was an engineer and Jason was a bit of an all round handyman and we have a few books in our small library that may be of some help."

"I would love to, I won't promise anything but it would certainly be a challenge to see what we can come up with."

"You probably noticed that a couple of our trucks are away out this morning, they are away to pick up more of those sheets that you saw around the farming area, we want to enclose the complete village with that high fencing as we had a problem at the start of the winter in that when the snow drifted the dog packs were able to gain access over the top of the electrical fencing and killed one of our bullocks and we want to stop that from ever happening again and to give us more security. You have I take it seen all over the village, what do you think?"

"I think you all have done a marvellous job in setting up the lifestyle you have and in protecting yourselves. If I was unsure before about wanting to join your community I am certainly sure now after seeing what you have all achieved and organised. I must also say that the people that you have managed to gather here at present are all very pleasant and friendly and helpful and I would be honoured to be let stay with you all."

"That is not even in doubt we had already said that the three of you were more than welcome to join us. I vote we all head back to the main house and get a cup of Mary's coffee and then we can see about getting the post hole digger into action and start getting posts cemented into the ground ready for the panels to be put up.

CHAPTER 7

FORTIFYING THE VILLAGE"

They all headed back to the house and had their coffee and then started loading the panel van they had with posts and cement and the digger and made their way over to the fencing adjacent to the completed farm fencing and started digging holes in the hard ground ready for the posts to be put into place with the quick drying cement. They worked until it was time for lunch and then returned to the monotonous grind of digging holes and dropping in the posts and cementing them into place. They decided that they would fit the dozen or so panels that were available while they waited for the trucks to return and then start digging again. By early afternoon they had run out of posts but kept digging the holes until the two trucks arrived back and unloaded their fencing panels and posts. They now split into two teams one mounting the panelling to the posts and the other continuing to dig holes and put in posts.

They continued until it was time to call a halt for tea and made their way back to the house and collapsed into chairs and nursed their sore and aching bones and sucked their fingers where the hammer had taken its toll along with the splinters that had to be now removed.

Those that were smart enough found out that there was sufficient water for them to have showers provided they did not hog all the hot water. Meanwhile the fire was stoked up to keep up with the demand for the hot water and eventually they all managed to have a shower before tea and then made their way home to their bedrooms to collapse into their beds and went straight to sleep.

The whole idea was to completely fence in the village and the farming area where the livestock were kept and where they grew their few vegetables. From the bridge right round behind the houses and fields until they came to the mill where they had built another gate across the road to secure that end of the street.

The village ran along side the river Graven and had the bridge with the security gate at one end and the Mill at the other and a single road with houses and cottages off it and the fields backed on to the back of the houses on one side and the other side the river ran along behind the houses except where the car park was opposite the main house and there the river was directly behind the car park itself. They thought that the river would be a good enough security barrier on its own as it ran quite deep and the banks on both sides of the river were fairly steep and not very negotiable.

They decided that as this was going to be a job they would work at until completed they would take in another large field adjacent to the existing enclosed fields of their farm so as to have more room for livestock. Luckily they had found more than enough fencing panels to complete the job at the Council supply yard. This hard work went on for nearly two months until the end of March until the fencing around the village was completed to everyone's' satisfaction and then they strengthened the two security gates at either end of the village.

By the time the fencing was completed everyone was thoroughly sick of the sight of fencing panels. The sight of primrose growing along the side of the main street and daffodils growing in clumps in the front gardens of the houses helped give the scene a normality that it had not seemed to possess before. Meanwhile life went on in the village and Peter and his helpers had managed to have the electrical generator fitted at the mill and it was producing electricity for them, granted it was a limited supply but they had managed to give everyone of the occupied houses a limited supply sufficient to run a fridge and a couple of low wattage lights.

The girls schooling progressed in fits of starts and stops, conducted by Joseph Epton the novelist much to the disgust of the three girls.

Unfortunately now that everyone had a bit more time on their hands it gave them time to think about loved ones lost and a lifestyle lost although that seemed the least of their worries as everyone seemed to like the lifestyle they had now built for themselves, but unfortunately everyone just had to work their way through their own worries and upsets as going to a Doctor for anti depressants was a thing of the past, probably not bad a thing either.

Another thing that was decided at one of their meetings was that Mary had too much to do cooking every day for so many people, although it was her own fault because her cooking was so good that everyone wanted to eat at the main house all the time. So it was decided to ask for a volunteer to help her in the kitchen and young Rosemary said she would love to do it as she loved cooking and working in the kitchen with Mary, who agreed that they already got on very well together and she was already a great help in the kitchen, so it was agreed upon. Rosemary then asked did that get her out of doing any more school work and it also was laughingly agreed upon to her complete delight.
The men had a discussion about the wisdom of mounting a trip to Cambridge to see what was happening at that commune there and see if women were really being abused and held as sex slaves for the enjoyment of some men and what would they do about it if it was true. A vote was taken which included everyone in the village and it was unanimously agreed that they would put together an expedition without much further delay to see what they could do about the situation.

Over the next few days it was decided to send two vehicles with six of the men to see what they could do. Those that were decided upon to go were John, Jason, Don Peter, Hal and Mike. The vehicles were stocked with supplies that would be enough to last the six of them for round trip of one week. For weapons everyone had their own personal hand-gun, hunting knife and either a rifle or shotgun and they also issued to each man three hand grenades and John, Mike and Don also opted to take a machine pistol each and two of the hand held rocket launchers, one in each vehicle and Rusty gave them lessons on how to use them and they also brought one reload for each. In John's opinion they would be well able to take care of themselves in just about any situation.

They set off the next morning at eight o clock to tearful goodbyes from the women, it was a dry day and the sun was shining. They found that the roads had deteriorated badly in the winter, especially since John had last driven down them on his was to Hunworth from London, nature was fast taking back its own, the roads had pot holes with grass growing in them and they even saw a couple of small trees starting to grow in the middle of the road, the grass was encroaching everywhere they looked. They had to stop a couple of times to cut up trees that had fallen on to the road and were blocking them, luckily they had brought a small chain saw with them just for such an occasion. By the time they were approaching the outskirts of Cambridge it was three in the afternoon and they stopped for a confab. It was decided that one of the vehicles with Mike, Hal and Peter would circle the town and come in from the other side and in the morning when they found the compound they would contact John and his party on the two way radios they had taken from the army base and creep in as close as they could get without being detected and wait for John to make the first contact and see how the situation progressed and play it by ear from there.

The other vehicle made off on its trip round Cambridge and John and his party settled in for the night and ate cold rations and drank lemonade from cans as they obviously did not want to attract attention by lighting a fire.

The next morning feeling the cold after what seemed to be a long night broken only by taking turns on guard, they set off in the general direction that John thought that the locals had taken up residence from his memory of where he had met them on the trip down from London. After picking their way through rubble for fifteen to twenty minutes they saw smoke up ahead and stopped to call Mike on the radio. After the second attempt Mike replied that his party were in position and could see a couple of men moving around outside a large house and would be waiting to see how they got on. John had decided to take the machine pistol with him rather than a rifle as he was not a very good shot with a rifle if it came to a shooting match.

He revved up the engine deliberately to let the locals know that they had visitors and drove towards the smoke they could see at the end of the street. As they approached they saw a couple of men come out of the house carrying rifles over their arms and one other man already in the street had a shotgun in his hand. They drew up beside them and John smiled at them and said.

"I came through here a year ago and you said that if I wanted to come back and join your group you would consider it."

"How many in your group asked one of the men who had an air about himself of confidence and acted as if he was the leader of the group."

"The three of us and two other blokes and three women and four young girls ranging in age from twelve to sixteen years. We spent the winter in a village and it was fucking miserable what with the weather, no proper heating and the bloody dog packs." Replied John gruffly. What about your group how many of you are there?"

The leader replied that there were four men and four women of varying ages and he boasted that they were living in the lap of luxury what with all the food available to them and the women and the girls they had it was a great life. "What age did you say the girls they had were and who owned them?"

"The girls are sixteen, fourteen and two of twelve is that about right Don." Asked John half turning round to his companions.

"Yes that is close enough." replied Don. "The eldest girl is mine the others belong to no one."

"Are you going to invite us in for a drink?" Asked John indicating the house.

"Sure but you leave your weapons outside."

"Sorry no can do, this baby goes to bed with me." replied John and indicating the machine pistol hanging at his side.

"Now that is not very friendly." Came back the growled reply from the leader.

"That is the way it is and the way it stays." Replied John.

The leader made a sudden grab for his rifle but John was too quick for him and swung the machine pistol up which he had already cocked and fired a burst at the man that hit him on his chest and down his left arm and shoulder and at the same time Don had got a shot off at the guy with the shotgun and hit him in the hand and arm, the third man was too surprised to do anything except look frightened and he quickly dropped his weapon and said don't shoot don't shoot!! There was the sound of a burst of firing from the side of the house in front of them and then they heard Mike shouting. "Don't worry I got the guy that was getting ready to have a go at you." Then he and his two companions appeared from the side of a house.

John turned to their prisoner. "Are there any more of you."

"No just the four women inside."

"Right lets go and introduce ourselves to the ladies."

The prisoner spoke up with a leer and said. "You will find they will cooperate with you they are well trained."

John walked over to the man he had shot. He did not look too good , he was unconscious and the blood was pumping out of his chest where obviously an artery had been hit. His companion was sitting slumped on the ground and leaning against the front of a car and was very white about the face and he was holding on to his left arm and cursing at them and looking murderous.

John walked over to the unconscious leader and took out his automatic hand gun and leaned over the unconscious leader and calmly shot him in the head. And then before anyone could react he walked over to the other injured man and shot him in the head as well. "We can't take any prisoners and there is no point in leaving them behind, alive and plotting against us in the future." And then he turned his weapon on their prisoner who saw what was going to happen and started to cry and proceeded to soil his pants as John shot him twice as it was obvious that the first shot was not fatal and it took the second shot to do the job.

His companions were shocked by the sudden brutality of the act.

"It was going to have to be done either now or later and it was more cruel to have a debate about it and then to shoot them in two hours time and have them suffer all the nightmare of expectation of the act, also we can not afford to leave live enemies behind us who may cause us grief later on in an act of revenge. This way it is over quickly and they had not much time to worry themselves about it, I know it is barbaric but you know that I am right. Right will we go inside and see what the situation is in there?"

His companions mentally shook themselves and followed John inside the house. When they got inside they could hear the sound of women crying in a room off to the left and they opened the door cautiously and peered inside before slowly going in. John was the first to go into the room followed slowly by the others. They found three women sitting in lounge chairs and all were crying and after a second glance they could see that all three of them were handcuffed to the chairs that they were sitting in. John spoke to them.

"Stop crying you are not going to be hurt by us, I promise you. Where are the keys for the handcuffs?"

"He has them." Came back the sniffled answer from one of the prisoners.

"Hal will you go outside and search our late friend and see if you can come up with the keys for these cuffs please."

Hal turned and without a word went out the door on his task.

On looking more closely at the three women he found that one of them was only a child of about ten or eleven, another was a woman in her thirties and the last person was a girl in her late teens or early twenties, it was hard to tell because of the tears and the hair that had become plastered over their faces in their stress All three of them were dressed only in flimsy nighties and had no shoes or slippers on their feet and all looked like they needed a good bath.

John went over to the women and crouched down on to his knees in front of them, he spoke to them softly. "Don't be afraid we will not harm you, we are here to rescue you and let you get away from this place. The men are all dead and will not bother you again!" He took a handkerchief out of his pocket and handed it to the oldest woman that he was speaking to. His other companions were standing around looking awkward and not knowing what to do with them selves. He spoke to his companions over his shoulder. "Would some of you mind searching the rest of the house to see if there is anyone else in the property."

The woman he was crouched in front of and was speaking too spoke up. "Alice is upstairs locked in one of the bedrooms, she was being punished for running away, she was free for two days this time before they caught her again, it was the third time she had tried to escape, they beat her." She started to cry again.

"There, there, you are okay now and we will soon have you out of theses cuffs."

Her two companions just looked at him and his friend wide eyed and obviously very frightened that they were out of the frying pan and into the fire.

"All of you listen carefully to what I am going to say and you can ask any questions that you want when I am finished. Firstly we will release you out of these restraints, then we will let you all have a hot bath and get you some new clothes that are more suitable, feed you and then you will have a couple of choices on what you want to do after that. Either you can go away on your own or together, we will supply you all with guns, food and transport and you can all go where ever you want to or you may elect to come with us back to our village and meet our wives and stay with us in our community which at the moment numbers about twenty people and include men, women and children and no one will ever bother you again, everyone has a say in their future and everything is done only after a vote is taken by the complete community and I can tell you that it is a good life that we have."

The woman started to reply and John said. "Hush don't speak or give us an answer now, lets get you all cleaned up and then you can make your decision." He turned to the women's two companions that were still weeping only more softly now that the initial shock had worn off to some extent and they were able to start to think that they might have a future away from this place.

"Do you understand what I am saying."

They nodded but still did not reply to him, they just continued to cry quietly. Mike came back into the room and said to John.

"We have found the other girl, she was upstairs in one of the bedrooms, she has been quite badly beaten with a strap or a stick her back is badly lacerated and she is barely conscious, I have left Don with her, at that point Hal returned into the room and had a key in his hand. His hands were all bloody from searching the corpse outside in the street.

"Jason can you and Hal take one of the vehicles and see if you can find a pharmacy and collect some bandages and some sort of antibiotic soothing cream for the injuries for the girl upstairs, Dettol for cleaning out her wounds and if you can find any antibiotic tablets or capsules as well as anything that you think may be useful and then can you find a store and find a selection of clothes for these four ladies that will keep them, going until they can go shopping themselves. Peter can you see if you can find out how to get some hot water in this place for the ladies to have baths. Mike you and I will see if we can prepare some hot food for us all and set up a table in the dining room if there is one in this place. Girls we will leave you alone for now so you can recover and talk or if you want to go upstairs to see your friend that is okay as well. There are six of us altogether and you have heard where we all are if you want any of us and can't find us just yell out."

John and Mike withdrew from what appeared to be a lounge room that the three women had been imprisoned in and left three still very frightened people behind them as they closed over the door just leaving it slightly ajar. They found the kitchen and started to hunt for what food there was in the larder, there was not much to be found, only booze so they went out to the remaining vehicle and brought in all of their supplies from it.

John found that Jason had been wise enough to take their walkie-talkie with him and called him on it and after several attempts got through to him.
"Jason can you find some food when you are out there and bring it back with you as well as there is very little here in the house and be careful of the dog packs and the last time I came through this town I saw some wild animals that had been let loose from the zoo so be careful."

"Do you want to say anything to me Mike about my executing those animals!"

" No, I will admit at first I was shocked but then I realised that you had no choice and I would have done the same myself, I just was a bit slow about making the decision

So no I don't condemn you for your decision nor do I think any less of you for what you did, actually I think it took a certain amount of courage and after all we do not have the luxury of a police force or any courts to punish them, so don't worry about it, there is no need to mention it again."

It took another hour and a half before Jason and Hal returned from their shopping trip. They came into the house laden with shopping bags from supermarkets, pharmacists and ladies clothing and shoe shops.

"We got some pairs of slippers to do them until we can get them to a shoe shop to get properly fitting shoes for them." said Hal.

"That was great." John replied to him. "Which bag is from the pharmacy?"

"This one." replied Jason as he indicated a carry bag.

"Thanks, I will take it upstairs." He proceeded upstairs to see the other girl whom he had not met yet, he called out when he got to the head of the stairs, Don where are you?"

John made his way to the room that Don's voice had replied from and found him sitting in a chair at the edge of a bed that contained from what he could see was a female figure lying on her stomach.

"Is she conscious?"

"Yes barely, she lapses in and out of consciousness."

"Does she know what has happened and that she is no longer a prisoner?"

"Yes I think so she has settled down a bit from what she was like when I first found her."

"Can you please go down stairs and ask the older woman if she feels up to coming up here to give me a hand to clean up her friend and to dress her wounds." John went over to the side of the bed where Don had been sitting holding her hand

"Alice can you hear me my name is John and I need to dress your wounds and clean them up for you, do you understand."

"Yes I can." Came back the low reply from the girl on the bed.

Just as John started to examine her wounds on her back the older woman from downstairs came hesitantly into the room carrying a basin of hot water.

John smiled at her and said. "Thanks for coming to give me a hand, just put the basin here at the foot of the bed." He tested the water and found it to be a bit too hot. "Can you please get me some cold water to help cool this down a bit." He indicated the basin and again smiled at her. "By the way what is your name as you know mine is John?"

The woman stopped as she was going out the door and replied in a soft voice. "Martha." and disappeared out the door. When Martha returned with a jug of cold water John put enough into the basin, trial and error until he judged it was not to warm to use to clean up Alice's back and then added a good dollop of Dettol to it.

"I know that was more than I required but I would rather have to much at this stage rather than too little." He rummaged in the bag of pharmaceuticals and found a roll of cotton wool and tore off a lump to use as a washcloth. "It was not just to give me a hand here that I wanted you for it was I thought more appropriate that a third party was present while your friend was half naked and under the circumstances I thought it was not appropriate for the third person to be one of my friends."

John then proceeded to gently wash the girls back with the mixture of Dettol and warm water and then gently tapped it dry with clean cotton wool and then after more searching the bag he found a couple of antibiotic creams and smoothed it on to her back where the lacerations were and then covered the wounds with dressings that were anti stick and would not pull at the wounds when they were being dressed. and then covered her back with sheets of gauze and lightly stuck them into place with surgical tape.

"Well the boys certainly did their shopping well they seemed to think of everything. Can you please sit with her for a few moments and I will fetch her a cold drink to help her swallow the antibiotics." John left the room and went downstairs to fetch her a cold drink of water. When he entered the kitchen he found that his companions had been busy putting together a meal for them all.

"How is she?" asked Peter.

"Well at least the wounds are now clean, but she has been cruelly abused." Replied John. Can someone fetch the other two girls into the kitchen here to have some food and see if you can get them talking to you about anything that works for you."

When John returned to the bedroom and the patient he found that they seemed to be talking together in low voices.

"Here we are, some cold water that I have brought you to help you swallow the antibiotics and also a couple of pain killers called Endone which are a form of morphine but this is not too strong a dose. Can I help you or would you rather have Martha help you?" Martha reached for the glass of water and the capsules and tablets and helped Alice to rise up slightly on the bed to take them. She sank back down again after taking the drugs with a sigh.

"We are going to leave you for a short time so that Martha can get cleaned up and changed and have something to eat, then we will return and bring you something light for you to eat, okay!"

John and Martha made their way downstairs and Martha collected some clothes from the shopping bags that she thought she could get into and then made her way to a bathroom and John told her. "We will see you downstairs in the kitchen." And he made his way downstairs.

When he walked into the kitchen he found that his companions were still making heavy going of it trying to get the girls to open up, he found out that their names were May and June and the youngest was June. They were picking at their food and were obviously still very much ill at ease. At least they had cleaned themselves up and had stopped crying for the moment but looked like it would not take much to start them off again.

"If you want to go upstairs to see your friend feel free to do so and please ask Martha to come down to join us for some food, also you two might like to stay with Alice until Martha rejoins you after she has fed herself." The two girls literally dashed out of the kitchen and up the stairs.

"These girls are that heavily traumatised that it is possible that they may not join us at the village but opt to go their own way, and frankly I don't think I would blame them, it will take a long time before they ever trust the male species again. Jason when we get back to the house would you mind bunking in with either Joseph, Don or Hal so a to free up one of the larger bedrooms and we will put four bunk beds into that room if the girls do decide to return with us."

"Sure no problem as long as whoever it is does not mind me snoring." Jason replied with a smile.

Hal spoke up and said. "You can move in with me if you don't mind although the room is a bit small."

"Yes it is I agree." Said John. "How about you and either Joseph or Don swapping rooms because their rooms are a lot larger."

"I will swap with you." volunteered Don. "My room is definitely the largest and I really do not need the extra space, it will suit me fine."

"Thanks guys it's just that if these women do decide to join us it might help them to feel more secure if they were all in the same room." John looked up and saw Martha standing at the door ready to enter but had waited for the men to finish their discussion.

"Come in Martha we were just talking about you and your three companions but I think we will leave it for a couple of days, I think it is too early on for you all after the traumas that you have all endured, the other thing was I think it would have been a good idea to move out of this house as soon as possible as it holds too many bad memories for you but I think your friend Alice is too ill to move for a couple of days and it would take too much out of her at the moment, do you agree?"

"Yes I do." Agreed Martha nodding her head as well.

"Fine, grab a seat and we will get you some food."

Don brought over to the table a plate with some sliced ham on it along with tinned three bean mix and tinned sliced pineapple and asked what she would like to drink.

"Some tea please." she answered with a strained smile.

The men just stared talking about back home and they would be glad to see their friends and in some cases their partners and about their village and the life they had made for themselves there.

Martha finished most of the food on her plate and said maybe she should go back upstairs to her friends.

Don spoke up and said. "Would she mind taking up some mixed tinned fruit for Alice as he thought that was probably as much as she would be able to handle for the moment and he gave her a plate of fruit and a spoon. She took it with a thanks and a soft smile and turned and went back upstairs without any further conversation.

John spoke up. "It is nearly four o clock and I think it is a bit late to do much more today so I vote that tomorrow we find a van and fill it up with the usual groceries ready for when we decide to move on back home, other than the usual jerry cans that we will put on the roofs of our vehicles is there anything else that we should add to our shopping list."

Peter said. "What about some more schoolbooks for the children because if these people decide to come with us it means that there are going to be three young girls needing schooling."

"Good idea and possibly some more D.I.Y. books as well if anyone can remember what we already have so as not to double up, possibly some books on gardening with an emphasis on vegetable gardening and electrical and plumbing and the usual seeds and I don't think clothes for the ladies will go astray either and the usual range of shoes. I think if we bring inside all our weapons and lock the doors and windows we should not need to post a guard and we are all pretty light sleepers anyway. They all went in search of a bed for themselves and brought three other mattresses upstairs for the girls to sleep on in Alices room and some blankets and pillows for them as well

John looked in on the women in their room and to tell them that they were all going to try and get some sleep and was there anything that they wanted before they said goodnight.

They said no they were all okay.

Just as he was going out the door John took his hand gun out of his holster and placed it on a chair and said it might make them feel a bit more secure to have a weapon in the room with them, just to make sure they don't shoot any of them in the morning and if they wanted to lock their door feel free to do so.

He was half way down the stairs when he heard the key turn in the door lock, he smiled ruefully as he tried to understand what those poor women must be going through. It didn't take a trained psychiatrist to work out their state of minds.

When John returned to the kitchen Peter raised his eyebrows in query at him.

"They have settled in for the night, I gave them my hand gun to see if it might give them an added sense of security and I heard them lock the bedroom door as I was going down the stairs, so be careful in the morning when approaching any of them, we don't want any accidental shootings. Any coffee left please before I call it a night,"

"You will never sleep if you stuff yourself with coffee." remarked Hal as he poured out a mug for John and put the pot back on the stove so as to keep the rest hot for any one else. "Sorry there is no milk, we forgot to bring any with us."

After they had talked for just over an hour on what they planned to do the next day, they decided to call it quits for the night and would try and get some sleep. They decided just in case to post a guard. Hal volunteered to take the first shift from now which was eleven ten pm to three in the morning and then John said he would take over from him until they all got up,

"Just wake me Hal when you want me to take over, I don't mind if it is earlier if you are having difficulty staying awake until three."

"No I will be okay, three will do fine, goodnight."

The five of them decided to split between two rooms and Hal would stay in the kitchen where it was reasonably warm from the stove.

When John was waiting for sleep to overcome him he mused that the next trip they went away he would bring Max with them as he would waken the dead if anyone came near them during the night and that way no one needed to go without sleep staying up to keep watch. The next thing he knew was Hal shaking his shoulder to waken him for his turn on watch. "Thanks Hal no problems I suppose."

"Other than one or two of the women wept all night long without a break, I also heard a couple of them, talking most of the night. They are awake still, or were up to a few moments ago. See you later around seven or there about's."

After Hal went off to grab some sleep he could hear one of the women crying and sobbing in the dead quiet of the night. The night passed uneventfully until dawn broke, then he could hear a blackbird outside announcing its arrival for the world. He decided that he needed a cup of his usual pick me up and he would make enough for the rest as most of them were coffee drinkers too except possibly Hal who had a preference to sweet soft drinks like Coco cola. Jason followed closely by Peter was the first to appear and soon the rest of them straggled in and they started to make some scrambled eggs from powdered eggs and put the last of the ham into the pan and fried it up until the smell of a fry was permutating throughout the house

John put some onto plates for the ladies upstairs and got a bowl of warm water to bathe Alice's back with and asked if someone would help to carry the plates of food upstairs. Peter volunteered and grabbed a couple of the plates and some cutlery and followed John upstairs. When they arrived at the closed door John knocked it and called out.

"Good morning ladies, breakfast has arrived can someone open the door as our hands are full carrying plates." There was a brief pause for about ten seconds and they heard some whispering and then someone made their way over to the door and unlocked it and swung it wide open. When the door opened Martha was standing there holding the door knob with one hand and John's gun with the other and they could see the other three girls all cuddled up together with their arms around each other and sitting on the bed.

John ignored the gun in Martha's hand and cheerfully asked them if they had slept at all, not letting on that he knew they hadn't as he made his way over to the bed and put the plates of food down on top of the doona and the bowl of water on the side table.

Peter put his plates and cutlery down beside the others and cheerfully said to them.

"Good morning all the sun is shining and the birds are singing and today has to be better than yesterday and then he turned on his heel and walked out of the bedroom without a backward glance.

"How is your back this morning Alice? I bet it is stiff and sore, well if you would allow me I will see to your dressings, I have brought warm water with me and I will just add some Dettol to it and then Martha and I will take off the old dressings, it should not cause you too much stress because of the type of dressings that I used yesterday, they should not stick too bad. Do you mind if I ask you to lay over on your side and if the rest of you would like to start into the food before it gets too cold, sorry it is powdered eggs but back home at the village we have some hens and we have the luxury of fresh eggs and not this powdered rubbish but beggars can't be choosers." John was aware he was gabbling but he was trying to act as normal as he could so as to put the girls at their ease because they still looked like frightened does' with their eyes seeming to stand out like a Chihuahuas and acting very skittery. Martha could I ask for your help, if you could ease off the dressings at the other side of the bed." At this request Martha went round to the other side of the bed and touched Alice on the shoulder and indicated and said that she should roll over on to her tummy. This she did and John carefully started to ease off the dressings, they came off without any problems and he was able to see the wounds for the first time since yesterday when he had originally dressed them.

They are I believe no worse and possibly a bit better but they are still looking very red and angry. Do you mind if I wash them with the Dettol and water in this bowl and then I will redress them again for you. Alice spoke for the first time.

"No I don't mind and thank you." She quietly murmured.

John with Martha's help washed her back and cleaned out the wounds and then smoothed on more of the antiseptic cream and put on more of the non stick sterile dressings and then covered her back with sheets of fresh gauze and taped them into place as he had done previously and she then sat up carefully in the bed holding a sheet to the front of her body. At that point John t reached over for one of the plates of food that no one had touched yet and put it into her lap and handed her a knife and fork. "Alice I have here for you more of the antibiotic capsules and two more of the morphine tablets, you need to take two of the capsules now, two more at lunch time and two before you settle down for the night, the two Endone tablets you can take anytime you want to or not at all, it is up to you but the antibiotics are most important that you do take as I have suggested. Bon appetite, if any of you ladies want to use the bathroom please feel free to do so How are you young June and you May is there anything I can do for you two? If any of you want to come down stairs or go outside please feel free do so, just don't wander too far and make sure you ask someone to give you weapons in case you run into any of the wild dogs. Some of us have chores we have to do in preparation for when we eventually leave here to go back home." He did not get any reaction from May but young June gave him a tentative smile, he then smiled at them all and made his way out the door and pulled it after him and headed back down stairs. This time he did not hear the key turn in the lock after he had left so he thought to himself at least that is some progress.

When he returned downstairs to the kitchen he found that Peter, Mike and Hal were getting ready to go out to find a van and fill it up with stores.

"We will see you later called out Mike as they went out the front door and down the steps."

"Thanks guys see you later when you get back, be careful."

Don said. "I think Jason and I will go and fill up our vehicle with petrol and see if we can find any jerry cans and fill them as well, they can go on the roof rack. We will also see what we can find in the way of groceries to fill up the back of the car, will you be okay on your own with the four ladies?" he joked with a smile.

"I will try and manage." replied John.

John decide to explore the house and see what if anything had the gang been gathering up since the world had changed so dramatically a year ago. He started at the top of the house and worked his way down to the kitchen, just leaving out the room where he heard the girls talking in low voices. Other than weapons of which there were quite a lot and some food, they seemed to have literally been living from hand to mouth and no forethought for the future at all. He heard the bedroom door open and someone going into the bathroom and the sound of running water in the bath and then silence descended on the house. He made himself the usual pot of coffee as what had been made for breakfast seemed to have been all drunk. When he finished his coffee he decided to go upstairs to check on the girls and see how they were. When he arrived outside the bedroom door he knocked and announced himself.

Shortly after the door was opened by young June and he saw that Martha was sitting on the side of the bed talking to Alice and June was missing so she must be the one in the bathroom. That is probably good, it must mean that she is starting to come out of her shell and personal private hell that she had seemed to be in.

"How goes it girls is there anything we can do for you?"

Alice smiled over at him and replied. "No thanks we were just talking about your offer to possibly take us with you or to let us go our own way, does that offer still stand?"

"Sure it does girls, but as I said take your time as we told the folks back at the village we would be away for seven days and that still leaves us with four to go, the others in my party are away out grocery shopping and what ever else takes their fancy, so there is only just me left behind for the moment. If you want to take the opportunity to take a walk outside and still feel nervous with six men around you who are strangers and you still have not made up your minds about us now would be a chance to get a bit of fresh air if you feel up to it and with no one around. Just take weapons from the kitchen where we have piled them all. Back at the village everyone carries a sheath knife, a revolver and either a shot gun or rifle at all times and that includes all the ladies, although the children make do with a hand gun and knife as sufficient for them, as the village is completely fortified and they don't have to worry about wild dogs or other animals. We are great believers in Murphy's law, shit happens even when it can't possibly happen so we take no chances specially with the ladies getting hurt. To change the subject how is your back?"

"It feels fine but it seems to be stiffening up a bit."

"That is to be expected, it means that it is starting to heal." How is May, is she starting to recover from her trauma at all, I heard her going into the bathroom which I thought was a good thing. I am heading downstairs, if someone could look in on her and maybe I will see you all downstairs, mind you Alice I wouldn't push it in your case, you might be better to leave it until tomorrow." He turned and went out of the door and headed for the kitchen and decided to put on the kettle in case anyone wanted a cup of tea because they were not coffee addicts like him. He heard the bedroom door open and then he heard young June calling out to May in the bathroom, obviously she had locked the door after her when she went in then he heard Martha calling out to her several times then the kitchen door which was ajar opened and June came in and said.

"Martha asked would you please come upstairs as she can not get any reply from May and the door is locked."

""Sure lead the way." He followed June up the stairs and found Martha standing outside the bathroom door and Alice standing in the entrance of their bedroom and holding on to the door frame for support.

Martha turned to him. "I can not get any reply from May and she has locked the door, can you get it open because I am worried?"

"Sure I can try, but maybe we should wait a bit longer, because if I burst open the door with her present traumatised state of mind it will not do her any good."

"No I really would like you to open the door as quickly as possible because there is no noise at all not even the sound of water from the bath."

"Okay, just give me a minute I saw a large screwdriver downstairs, I would prefer to try it first rather than smashing down the door because of her state of mind and you will have to go in first to reassure her. I will only go in if you want me in there for any reason." He turned round and dashed downstairs to try and find the screwdriver. After a quick search he found it on one of the workbenches in the kitchen and ran back up the stairs where the others were all waiting for him with anxious faces.

He levered at the side of the lock where the tongue of the lock went into the door frame and quickly got the door to open and Martha pushed past him and went inside and then he heard her cry out.

"Oh my God! Please help quickly! She has hurt herself!"

John quickly go up off his knees where he had been crouching from opening the door and followed Martha inside. He saw at a glance that May was in the bath and the water was all red from blood, he quickly turned round to June and said.

"You had better wait outside until Martha comes out to you." And he went inside and closed the door behind him leaving a stunned June outside and Alice asking.

"What has happened?"

When he went back inside he saw Martha bending over the bath and trying to get a grip of May by the shoulders to see if she could lift her out of the bath. There was blood everywhere and he saw a razor blade lying on the floor alongside the bath and saw cuts on both of her wrists. He pushed past Martha and tried to find a pulse behind her ear at the side of her neck but there was none.

"If you can grab her by the legs I will take her shoulders and we can lay her out on the floor. Saying that he immediately got her under the armpits and lifted her and Martha had her by the feet, they got her out of the bath and laid her down alongside the bath and again he tried for a pulse but to no avail and he noticed that her wrists had stopped pumping blood as well which meant that her hearty had stopped beating, she was gone. Martha was sobbing and he took her in his arms and tried to comfort her but she was terribly distressed. He helped her to her feet and grabbed a couple of towels and helped her out of the bathroom.

Outside the door Alice and June were waiting on the landing white faced and expecting the worst.

"I am so sorry she has taken her own life by cutting her wrists, there is nothing we can do for her. I am afraid she just did not have the strength to go on, things had finally proved to be to much for her. I am sorry we did not come here even a week sooner and this may not have happened. When the others return we will give her a proper burial if you would like that. In the mean time, if you Alice could take young June into the bedroom, Martha and I will clean up a bit and join you as soon a possible and he ushered the two other girls into the bedroom weeping and hugging each other for comfort. John took Martha by the arm and helped her downstairs and helped to clean the blood from her hands and arms and face where she had rubbed it with her hands in her distress.

"I am afraid there is not much you can do to salvage that blouse I will have to ask you to remove it and when you go back upstairs you can put on another one. He then tried to get as much of the blood off himself as possible and like Martha his shirt was completely covered so all he could do was to remove it and try and get as much of the blood off his hands as possible. He found a clean shirt in one of their bags in the kitchen and asked Martha.

"Are you okay to go back upstairs to join the other girls."

"Yes." She replied still sobbing.

On the way upstairs he grabbed some glasses from the kitchen and a bottle of scotch and one of vodka that there was an abundance of lying around as that seemed to have been the main occupation of the gang, drinking heavily everyday and night. Then abusing the women, he thought they all could do with a good stiff drink because of the shock.

He opened the bedroom door and found Alice with tears streaming down her face and at the same time trying to comfort June who was crying her heart out in uncontrolled shuddering sobs. He brought Martha over to the other two and set her down on the bed.

"We had to remove Martha's blouse as it had been covered in blood do you have another one she can wear Alice."

Alice nodded and got up and went over to a chest of drawers and opened the second one down and pulled a blouse out of the drawer and handed it to Martha who pulled it on over her shoulders but was still too distressed to button it up.

"I really am sorry girls for what has happened, I have brought up with me some drinks which it maybe a good thing for you to have some for the shock but it is up to you, again no one will force you do anything against your will from now on as I promised you all."

The sobs were quietening down and Alice asked for a drink of Vodka and Martha said she would have the same. June asked was she allowed any?

"Yes I think a little drop for you will not do you any harm, just drink it slowly and a little at a time."

To try and take the girls minds of the terrible tragedy he suggested to Alice that he dress her back for her, she agreed although it was obvious that what had happened had upset her badly.
John went downstairs and obtained the usual bowl of warm water and added the disinfectant to it and she removed her blouse and undid her bra. straps and laid down on her face on the bed. He gently removed the old dressing and examined the wounds for any infection.

"This is looking good, the angry look has left it all and it is scabbing over nicely."

He proceeded to gently dab the wounds with the mixture of disinfectant and water and to pat them dry with cotton wool and to smooth some of the disinfectant cream over the long wounds and replace the dry non-stick dressings and this time he thought that he could leave off the sheets of protective gauze.

"Those are looking good, just try and not stretch your back too much for a while until the scabs crust over properly, we don't want the crusts to crack as that will cause them to probably ooze a little." He bundled up the old dressings and took them and the bowl of water out of the room and downstairs to be disposed of.

He had just disposed of the soiled dressings when he heard the sound of a motor engine and then one of their Range Rovers appeared down the street and heading towards him. The vehicle stopped beside him and Hal alighted from the drivers seat.

"You are just in time to help me dispose of an ugly chore." Greeted John to Hal as he explained what had happened in his absence that morning.

Hal was naturally upset. "Does it never stop the ugliness in this bloody world?" he muttered in shock at the news.

"Can you give me a hand if you don't mind to bring the body downstairs and out the back where we can bury it after we have cleaned up the bathroom so the girls can use it, unfortunately there is only the one bathroom in the house!"

The two men went back inside and carried the body downstairs and wrapped it in a sheet and laid it out on the lawn and then went back inside to see if they could clean up some of the mess from the blood in the bathroom. Using rags torn off sheets they cleaned up the blood as best as they could using them and plenty of water, after they had done their best they went outside to see if they could dig a grave for May in the back garden. When they went outside to bury her there were at least three large rats trying to gnaw their way through the sheet to get at the body and they had to be chased off before they could get on with the job. They choose a spot under a cherry tree up against the back fence. It was tough going trying to get the spade through the frosted ground which was as hard as a rock, they took turns until the job was done and then sweating like pigs even though it was still so cold they lowered her into the grave they had dug and filled in the soil on top of her and then went back inside to clean themselves up before the girls saw them.

While Hal was taking his turn in the bathroom John put on the kettle once again so as to make some coffee which he poured into two mugs and added a good dash of whiskey to them and handed one to Hal and then sprawled into a chair.

"Have you noticed that the rat population has started to increase a lot or is it just my imagination."

"I have and the brutes have become a lot more aggressive and do not seem to have any fear in them and they are mostly huge. A couple I saw when I was out this morning were nearly as big as a small dog!"

"I think we should think about stocking up on rat traps and baits before we return because the bastards seem to be everywhere you look." replied John.

At that moment the three girls appeared in the kitchen and without a word being said Hal got up and poured out three more mugs of coffee and added a dash of whiskey to them as well and handed them over to the women who sat down at the kitchen table.

Martha spoke up and thanked him for the drinks and Alice smiled a wain smile in thanks as well

"We have been talking between ourselves and listening to your conversations between yourselves as well and have come to the conclusion that if you will still have us we would like to take you up on your offer to return to your village with you if you don't mind and if the offer is still open?" Martha tentatively asked and the other two nodded in agreement.

"Of course you can, it is just we did not want to put any pressure on any of you especially after what you had all been through, it was hard for us as strangers to gain your trust and to reassure you that you were not jumping from the frying pan into the fire in other words the same situation or worse. Replied John with a smile at the girls to try and take some of the seriousness out of his words.

I think if everyone is in agreement we will head home tomorrow if you feel your back is up to the trip Alice, we can give you some cushions to pad your back with up against the seat."

"The others should be returning soon, it is nearly twelve noon and then we can have something to eat." said Hal joining in to the conversation. "How is your back Alice, it is good to see you up and about even in these circumstance?"

As if the others had heard him they heard the sound of vehicle engines and when they looked out the front door they saw the others had returned in two vehicles, one large panel van and the other Range Rover. The four remaining members of their party alighted from the vehicles and made their way over to join them at the front of the house. Martha greeted them.

"Come inside and we will see if we can find anything for breakfast." She turned on her heel and went back inside, followed by the other two girls.

Mike raised his eyebrows and smiled at John as much as to say. things were starting to look up and went inside after the three girls followed by everyone else.

When they had seated themselves at the table and brought in to the kitchen some more chairs John explained what had transpired in their absence. The four men who had just returned expressed their sincere heartfelt sorrow to the three remaining girls and that brought back a few of the tears. They also expressed their delight at the news that they had decided to return with them and go to the village.

"Bye the way John have you noticed the rat population have increased both in size and volume. One of the buggers had a go at me this morning in the supermarket and tried to bite my boot in dispute over some grocery item that we both wanted and I actually had to kill it as it would not back off." remarked Mike as he took a drink of his coffee and whiskey that the four returning men had opted for when offered it.

"Yes I was just saying before you returned that we are going to have to scour the shops for rat traps and baits before we leave tomorrow, would you mind going back out after you have had some food and see if you can find any to take back with us!"

"No problem at all, I suppose I had noticed the increase in the rat population, it just had not registered with me."

CHAPTER 8

THE INCREASE IN THE RAT POPULATION.

Thew next morning everyone stoked themselves up on a good breakfast of powdered scrambled eggs, fried ham and tinned sausages and cheese and of course the usual coffee and tea which the ladies seemed to prefer. Before they left they went outside to the back garden to the grave that Hal and John had dug and had a quite ceremony for May and Hal planted a cross that he had made and had carved her name on.

They all said their good buys in their own different ways and then took their leave from the sad place the garden had become. The three remaining girls expressed their gratitude to the men for what they had done for May.

Alice went with Hal in his Rover sitting in the front passenger seat well propped up with pillows and Martha and June went with John in his vehicle and the other four men crowded into the van which had four seats in it in the front of the cargo area.

The back seat of Hal's and Alice's Rover was full of rat baits and traps that they had found and packed in there. Their first call after leaving the house was to the shops to outfit the three women in new clothes, John drew the vehicle up to the front of Mark's and Spencer's a large shop that was part of a chain of shops that sold all sorts of clothing for both men and women and shoes and all sorts of accessories.

"Right ladies I want you to go in to the shop and pick out complete outfits for yourselves including shoes and boots for both Summer and Winter, start from the skin out as I am sure you want to rid yourselves of any clothes that may remind you of your experiences over the last year. We will go in with you to guard you from any dogs or vermin, so lets go, just use shopping bags to put everything in"

The girls spent a good hour in gathering up all that they might need for the near future, the therapy of shopping and the thought that they were leaving all of the past behind them was as good as a tonic for the three women.

On the way back to the village they seemed to notice that really the rat population seemed to have exploded since their trip out to Cambridge. After travelling for two hours they reached the outskirts of the village and drew up at the bridge gate and as usual they found Bobbie sitting there waiting on them on his self imposed task that he seemed to do for everyone that was absent from the village and away on a trip.

"Good to see you all back safe." He shouted out to them as they drove past him and on down the road to the main house. When they drove up to the front door everyone who seemed to live in the village seemed to erupt out of the front door and greeted them, the girls to greet their men with hugs and kisses and tears of relief to see them returned all safe and sound and the unattached people just seemed happy to see them.

John kissed Anne and gave her a big hug and then turned to Bobbie who was standing near by with his usual big grin and rumpled his hair and said. "I see we are going to have to find you more work to do, you obviously have nothing to do that you are able to sit there at that gate every day all day."

Bobbie just grinned even wider.

John introduced the three newcomers and ushered them inside and when he noticed Alice's drawn face said that Alice had a sore back from an injury and needed to sit down before she collapsed. Immediately everyone was all concerned and helped her inside and found a big comfy chair for her to sit in and got her seated and propped up with cushions. Mary went into the kitchen followed by Rosemary to make drinks for everyone, they ranged from water, soft drinks, beer and spirits and tea and coffee, so that everyone was satisfied.

John called for order and suggested that, Lisa, Poh and the new arrival June all move into the room with the four bunk beds and Martha, Alice and Rosemary move into the three bunk room as that was probably the best sleeping arrangements and it gave the three children more freedom to get up to mischief, the latter statement he took the sting out of his words with a smile at them to their denials privately he hoped that the other young girls would help in the mental heeling process for June and Rosemary was such a friendly girl he hoped that her presence would help Alice and Martha. Although from what he could see of Hal's attentions to Alice he might have some thoughts in helping out there and she seemed not to be oblivious to them.

Over the next couple of days things settled back into the normal routine and the newcomers seemed to settle down and everyone seemed to have taken them under their proverbial wings when they heard their horrific stories from the way they had been treated over the last year.

By this time it was the end of March and the usual meeting was called in the main house with everyone in attendance and the usual list of things were made out for the next scavenging trip for supplies. Also the question was asked if there were any requests to change the sleeping arrangements by changing rooms or moving out to one of the cottages. There were no changes asked for in this area although he noticed a look pass between Hal and Alice and thought with an inward smile, that situation will change before long

He also asked if anyone had noticed the increase in the rat population. Everyone agreed that they had noticed the increase, but the village itself was not too bad because Max and Jessie seemed to have a great time in catching them and had made it into a game they never tired of. John suggested that the situation was going to get worse and possibly dangerous as the bite from rats was never good even at the best of times and one did not know what disease they were harbouring now since the death and the dogs would need to be examined frequently for any rat bites to catch them before they went septic. Also it may be a good idea to keep their eyes open on their trips for a cat possibly one with a litter of kittens although all the cats seemed to have gone feral by now. Also every trip from now on they would have to include on their lists were rat traps' and baits.

Another idea he had he wanted to explore with those who had electrical knowledge if those men could stay behind after the meeting was over. The young girls using Rosemary as their spokeswoman asked if they could possibly find and I pods or disc players on their trips along with discs and batteries to give them some music. They were told it would be made a priority on the top of the list that sent them into giggles of gratitude. And made the adults all smile. The meeting eventually broke up with everyone who wants a say having one and everyone went their separate ways feeling satisfied with the results. Martha and Alice came over to John after the meeting and again thanked him for bringing them back to the village as for the first time since they recovered from the sickness they felt safe and secure and felt they had some real friends that were not out to exploit them. John told them they were more than welcome.

After the meeting was over Tom Fielding who was a qualified electrician and Jason and Mike Thornton who both claimed to have some basic knowledge of electricity stayed behind and came over to John and also Bobbie was asked to stay.

"Thanks for staying behind guys, I would like to run over an idea I have in the back of my mind and see if you think it has any merit for defending the village from a possible rat infestation which has the potential to be disastrous for us all. It is really an extension of the electrified fence that we were using at the start for keeping the livestock in and the dog packs out. He pulled up a sheet of paper and started sketching on it.

"As you know the ordinary electrical fence is no good for keeping the rats out because they just walk under it for a start. What I was wondering was, do you know the sheets of heavy duty steel wire that are done up in squares that builders bury in to the concrete slabs they pour for flooring to keep the concrete from cracking and acts also as a reinforcement and the wire sits on plastic pegs about two inches off the ground and supports the mesh and lets the concrete pour through so that the mesh finishes up in the middle of the slab, well if we laid a carpet about three feed wide back from the fence line and propped the mesh up on those pegs and wired the electric fencing kits to it would that electrify the mesh enough kill any rats that venture to stand on it on their way over to the fence where they hope to gnaw their way in."

Bobbie spoke up "Certainly the steel mesh would probably conduct the electricity but I think it will only give them a nasty shock I don't think it will be enough to kill them." he looked over to Tom for his views.

"No it wont kill them and I don't know how strong the shock would be, even if we diverted the power from the Mill that we are generating I do not think it would be enough to kill them because of the large areas that we would want to electrify and that would leave your fridges without power because we do not generate enough electricity to do both."

Jason spoke up and said. "What if we brought some of those high powered generators home that we see in plant hire yards and brought them inside our fence line and drilled holes in the fences and lead the wires outside and hooked the ends of the wires up to the mesh and switched them on if we were under an attack from the rats and looked like being overrun and for normal use we hook up all the electrical fence kits that we can get our hands on and leave them permanently switched on, it may be enough to keep them away and we have the others for an emergency if the going gets tough and every so often we can switch on the generators just to give them an occasional fry to reinforce the situation in their minds."

Tom said. "That would do the trick for the fence line then we only have to do something about the river as rats can swim and climb up the bank and overrun us from there.

"I think we just do the same for along the river bank and mount a couple of powerful search lights along the river to help keep an eye on the situation there. We will also require a method of being able to switch on all the generators from the house so we don't have to put anyone into danger from having to go out and switch them on individually." Said John.

"A good idea." said Tom. "But I think we need to take that idea further and have switch on points all over the village and out at the farm so that the matting can be charged by anyone who sees a dangerous situation developing and can act on it with out losing time running back to the main house to do it. We also possibly could do with a few watch towers built along the fence line so we can see over the fencing, because at the moment we can't do that because the fencing is too tall. Also the batteries for the electrified cattle fencing would need to be moved over to our side of the fencing for ease of changing flat batteries without putting someone in danger outside the fence. And we would need some sort of anti surge protectors on them so when we switch on the main generators we do not destroy the batteries from the cattle fencing, we are just adding to the power available which is a plus and we are not substituting one power source for another, it would actually boost the power output into the mesh."

Everyone agreed that the ideas put forward may solve the problem of keeping the rats out of the village.

It was decided to send out expeditions over the next week to bring back the generators and the steel mesh and the spacing pegs as soon as possible so they could implement the scheme immediately. Starting the next day they sent out their double axle trucks to look for and bring back as much off the mesh as possible and two men were sent out with each vehicle They were able to send out three Range Rovers along with the two trucks and that left just Bobbie that was left behind but it was explained too him that he was needed for his farm duties, much to his disappointment. Over the next five days they brought back fourteen of the large generators and ten trucks loaded with the steel mesh and bags of the spacing pegs and wire to tie the pegs on to the wire so it could not be shifted with the weight of any rats that climbed on to it.

The generators were spaced out along the perimeter of their fencing. Even with the fifteen generators they felt that they were short by about six for the main fence line and about a further eight were needed for the river side of the village so the Range rovers were sent out further afield to see if they could find what they wanted. Eventually after searching as far away as Kings Lynn, Cambridge and Norwich they found what they needed. Over the next month the system was completed and tested and everyone felt that it was a good job done and only just in time because the attacks by the rats were starting to prove a lot more determined and frequent and Mike got a bad bite on his shoulder where a rat had sprung at him when he was busy laying the mesh, but luckily a good strong dose of antibiotics and with a good scouring out of the wound he did not suffer any infection that did not clear up after a couple of days. It actually got that bad they had to have someone with a shotgun guarding those working at the mesh towards the end of the job.

They had the electrified cattle fencing kits all connected and up and running and they were generating quite a good charge just from the batteries alone. The generators they had not run yet as a deterrent because they wanted to keep that as a surprise up their sleeves but at present the rats were not game to run the gauntlet over to the wooden fencing and getting numerous shocks from the mesh. all the way over.

A few rats were to be found lying dead on the mesh were they had had so many shocks that their nervous systems could not survive and they had died. As far as everyone was concerned that was a bonus.

Unfortunately it was decided at a village meeting that they now required a permanent roving fence patrol twenty four hours a day and they had completed the last of the watch towers along the fence line. It was again voted on how long the tour of duty was to last for the fence patrols and the men decide to make the duty last for two weeks at a time, with two men on each tour at a time. The two men did a day shift and then swapped with the two on night shift for a week at a time on each shift and they soon settled down to the routine.

Over the next three weeks everything seemed to go along quite smoothly, the two dogs seemed to be able to keep any rats that found their way in under control along with all the rat traps they had set up all over the village, they were still sending out at least one scavenging trip per week, no word yet on any tame cats, that they could bring home. Summer appeared to be on its way with the start of May arriving.

The three new arrivals had settled in very well and were definitely now a part of the village.

Bobbie had always had the young girls helping with gathering the vegetables from the vegetable garden, collecting the eggs from the hen house and milking the cows and now that young June had joined them it now meant that he had three helpers, as the girls did these chores every morning before breakfast and school work that took up the remainder of their mornings. He and Poh had always been close, when she had first arrived she seemed to look to him for that extra support that she needed, but as time has gone on she has really gotten quite close to him and was to be found at the farm every day after lunch helping with the animals and anything that needed doing, it was not the first time someone had gone to the farm for whatever reason and found the two of them happily digging the vegetable garden and chatting away nineteen to the dozen. She had become a part of the farm, it seemed to just happen quite naturally and she obviously loved working there.

Hal and Alice asked could they move into one of the cottages. They moved from the main house in the middle of May and everyone treated it as a holiday and helped them to move their few possessions and Mary cooked a special meal in their honour and everyone got a little tipsy from the amount of wine that was drunk.

At the village meeting at the start of June someone suggested how about seeing if they could rig up a radio to see if they could contact anyone and find out how the rest of the world was doing It was decided that on the next trip into one of the major towns in the area to see if they could scrounge up the equipment required including a radio mast and to look in the largest book shop to see if they could find any books on amateur radios and the building and running of them. Until now they had been lucky with any illnesses or injuries even though they did have a third year medical student, a pharmacist and a qualified nurse in amongst their numbers but it was felt that they should make a more concentrated effort to gather up medical supplies and to try and stock a proper surgery / hospital in one of the smaller houses in the village in case it was ever needed, so medical books went on to the list along with the radio books and whatever else they thought they may require. It was decided to make the next trip a two vehicle trip one Rover and one dual axle truck and that they would send out two men and their partners in the vehicles as four men going out at one time put too much of a strain on their resources if any thing happened in the village and they required all the firepower they could muster up.

The rats continued to be a problem and they had to put on the generators one afternoon when they seemed to be gathering up in numbers to attack the village outside the fence around the farm area, after about a hundred fried themselves on the mesh they seemed to loose interest and then decided to see if they could gain access to the village from the river, but again there was not too much of a strain put on their defences as the bank up to the village from the water was fairly steep and the few rats that made it to the top the mesh took care of them along with a few shotgun blasts picking off any large numbers swimming across. They thought that when the snow arrived with the winter they may have their work cut out for them.

The following day Tom Fielding and his partner Mary and Brian Brooks and Joanne took off on the latest scavenging trip. They took with them one of the double axle vehicles and a Panel van. They made their way to Kings Lynn and Brian and Joanne headed for one of the towns large book shops and soon found the books that they were wanting about amateur radios and the setting up of a radio station, also they found a large book on homeopathic medicine and a book called, How to make medicines from the fields and hedgerows. They then made their way to one of the local pharmacies and started carrying out anything they thought they might require to set up a clinic including all the bandages that were in the place and dressings and creams and antibiotics and a blood pressure machine complete with cuff, thermometers, diabetic testing kits and Insulin, and found a couple of books on medical diagnostics. They still had not found any literature on medical procedures and how to carry them out. They decided to look in a couple of doctor's surgeries and also the local library.

They did find some items of interest in the surgeries but they eventually hit pay dirt in the local library in the medical section. There were heaps of books on medical procedures covering everything from childbirth to tonsillitis to appendicitis and anything else you could think of. They decide to complete filling the panel van with the usual food items from a couple of the smaller grocery shops as they had by now fairly well stripped the supermarket they had been in the habit of going to. After they had the van full to bursting they went in search of Tom and Mary and found them at a local D.I.Y electrical shop They went inside to join them and found Mary sitting on the floor playing with a cardboard box and making cooing noises at it. When they got closer they saw she had some kittens it the box along with the mother cat who was looking very alert but was not for budging when her kittens may be in danger although she did not appear too vicious, just growling from the back of her throat at them. Mary was delighted with her find, and Tom had gathered up a selection of equipment and a couple of books as well.

"Hi folks it looks like we have everything we may need including Mary's four little friends and Mother. I have the makings of a couple of huge aerials outside on the back of the double axle and along with this lot I hope it will do." Brian and Joanne gave them a helping hand to carry outside and load his trophies onto the back of the truck, along with the cat and kittens and they went inside the cab. They decided that they had enough except to see if they could take back with them some of the usual jerry cans of petrol, so they made their way over to a car parts store and stripped it of all the jerry cans they could find and made their way to the nearest garage and pumped them all full of gas and loaded them onto the back of the truck. They made it back to the village just as dusk fell and Bobbie let them in through the security gate at the bridge and they made their way down the street to the main house to be greeted by people coming out of the house to see how they had got on.

Everyone was tickled pink with the kittens and mother cat, the ladies took them inside to fuss over them. They managed to get help to unpack the van and flat bed truck. They unpacked everything except the aerial parts that they left on the truck until it was decided where to try to build the radio station as they had taken to calling their proposed construction. Everything else was unpacked and carried into the appropriate storage rooms.

They decided over tea that evening that they would set up the radio station in a corner of the lounge where there was an alcove with a settee in it and just move the seating out to somewhere else in the lounge. They had Brian Brooks build a work table or bench to put the equipment on, it took him no time at all to build it. Over the next two weeks the men used all their spare time to assemble the radio mast which was about one hundred and twenty feet tall round the back of the house, and to tie it into place securely with stay wires and to lead the wiring from the mast into the lounge at the work station for the radio and in setting up the equipment.

At last the day dawned when they tried the radio for the first time, everyone who was not doing some chores were present in the lounge and immediate area for the switching on of the radio. It was decided that they would put Don Whiteside in charge of the radio because he knew a little about it from his youth spent in the navy when he had actually worked a radio on a destroyer.

They had given themselves a name or handle as truckies used to call it for them selves. "New Haven". Also they did not want to use the name of the village because they did not want to be too specific as to their whereabouts until they knew more about whoever the managed to contact. After nearly an hour they had not had any luck in contacting anyone on any of the wave bands, so they decided to call it quits for the day.

Because Hal was a third year medical student he was the nearest thing they had to a doctor, the community asked him and Alice if they would mind putting the medical centre in to one of the rooms in their house. They did not mind so it was arranged for Brian to go down and to build shelving in the room that they had decided to use as a surgery. When all the shelving was built, a reasonably sized desk was found to move in to the room as well along with a swivel chair the place had started to look the part. The next trip into one of the towns it was decided to get a proper hospital style bed for the surgery and also another couple of hospital beds for one of the bedrooms that they had decided to make into a ward if anyone had to be immobilised in bed due to an injury or illness. Beth came down to help move all the drugs and medicines in and to put them into some sort of order on the shelving, as a qualified pharmacist she knew more about what way things should be stored and packed away and what should be beside what, also Anne as qualified nurse came as well to see if she could be of any help. Also all the medical books that they had been able to find on their scavenging trips were brought into the surgery as well along with any equipment they had brought back.

Hal was asked if he would mind opening a surgery every Friday morning in future so that people would get used to it being there and a loud bell was put outside for anyone to ring in an emergency if he was not at home and someone required his medical attention urgently.

After the surgery was set up everyone in the village said they felt as if they now had some security for the future although they were well aware that Hal's qualifications were lacking in that he was not a fully qualified doctor but they were still happy for what they felt he could do.

The radio station had picked up some chatter from the continent somewhere, possibly France because of the language being used but no one could speak French so it was ignored except for an occasional listen to in case they managed to find an English speaker but so far over the last three weeks that had not happened. Meanwhile the search went on.

It was now the fourteenth of July the middle of summer and other than one of the girls getting a bit of sunburn the surgery had not been used since it was set up. They decided that they would send out a team to see if they could gather in a few more head of livestock including a young bull if they could find one also some more sheep and pigs. So a party was put together with Bobbie in charge and they hitched on the two horse floats onto the back of a couple of the rovers and set off to see what they could find. Over the next week they managed to gather in four sows, one of which was suckling a litter of eight young piglets and three bullocks and a bull, he was a bit older than they had originally wanted but at least he seemed docile enough. They had eventually spotted some sheep up on the top of a hill about two miles away but had been unable to get near them. It was decide that the next day they would bring a couple of the horses with them to see if that would give them a bit more manoeuvrability. They got themselves to within approximately a mile of the flock of sheep and built a pen to help channel the sheep into the back of the horse floats. That was if they manage to drive them down to where they had prepared the pen, Rosemary along with John who had become quite proficient on horseback after his lessons from the girls set off in a roundabout route to see if they could drive the flock back to the waiting vehicles and horse floats. After a ride of some twenty five minutes they eventually found themselves behind the flock of sheep and the sheep between them and the vehicles. They rode towards the sheep and shouted out at them to drive them back to the cars, but all they managed to do was to scatter the flock all over the place. After their third attempt they managed to guide more by good luck than good management a group of three sheep back to the waiting men and the vehicles, after much shouting and swearing they got two of the sheep loaded and the third one got away. They decide to have lunch and the food was unloaded from the vehicles and they found that Mary had made some sandwiches and sent a freshly baked fruit cake and plenty of soft drinks and several packets of biscuits that tasted still fresh even after the time lapse of eighteen months since everyone had take ill and the world as they knew it had ceased to exist and only about one in every million surviving the illness which they had found with questioning everyone had lasted it seemed a mandatory five to six days. After lunch they decide to try once again to round up some more of the sheep. They spent the whole afternoon getting themselves into a lather and more and more short tempered until at the end of the afternoon just when they were about to give up the sheep seemed to tire of the game and trotted in a reasonable fashion down to the vehicles and they managed to secure ten of them along with the two captured early on that morning, one of the sheep appeared to be a ram and that along with the sheep at home gave them a reasonable sized flock. Bobbie came over to John and he had a piece of paper in his hand that he had been scribbling on.

"These animals captured today give us now at the farm, six dairy cows, twelve bullocks, one bull, thirty sheep, two rams, eight sows, two bores. eight piglets and an assortment of hens that I have no idea of how many." He announced with a pleased grin.

"I reckon that should be more than enough for our needs." Announced John to anyone who cared to hear him. They packed up and set off back home. When they arrived back they went to the farm to let the animals loose in with the other sheep that they already had.

Bobbie said they would soon calm down when they mixed in with the other sheep and found that they did not have to keep fleeing from dogs and rats trying to make a meal of them all the time.

That night after some hilarious stories vastly inflated with facts far from the truth at John's and Rosemary's expense at their attempts at herding the sheep they all relaxed with a couple of drinks sitting around the fire which they still kept going even though it was summer, everyone liked the effect of the fire and said it had a soothing effect on them. Rusty spoke up and said that he was so glad that everyone thought it was worthwhile in keeping the fire lit as tomorrow he was starting to organise another couple of week s of wood cutting for the coming winter. Most of the village came to the main house every night and listened to some music that the girls played on their disc players and relaxed with a few drinks and sat beside the log fire and discussed the things that they were going to have to do and in what priority.

Rosemary seemed to be enjoying her time in the kitchen as Mary's helper / apprentice and said she was glad to get back into the kitchen as her bum had become to soft from not enough riding and she was sore. A couple of the men volunteered to rub some lineament on it for her. Amidst laughter the offers were declined.

The next morning a team was put together and they went out of the village with the two double axle flat bed vehicles to a wood just over three miles away to start cutting up logs for the winter. After a hard mornings work and a harder afternoon they finally filled both the flat bed trucks to capacity and made their way back to the village to unload both the vehicles. They went to the furthest house that was occupied and filled up the wood storage shed to capacity and then to the next house and so on until by the time they had filled the shed for the third house they had emptied both the trucks. They made their individual ways to their homes and a hot bath before going for tea at the main house as arranged beforehand. When they managed to eventually get to the main house for tea they were nearly out on their feet as the hot baths had relaxed their muscles and they were just plain tired from the hard work. They ate their tea and then those that lived in their own houses made their way home and collapsed into bed.

The next morning they all ate breakfast together and collectively groaned about their aches and pains and compared notes. Mary said she had never heard so much groaning about a little work in all her days. Still she filled them all up with a good hot breakfast and sent them on their way with a packed lunch. It seemed to take a while until their muscles loosened up and they got properly into the swing of things, but eventually the groans became less and the work became more. At the end of the day repeated what they had done the previous day and went to the individual houses and filled their timber sheds up with the cut logs. They had tried to make the logs all of a uniform size that they knew would fit both the fire places and the ranges for cooking on. Again they made their way over to the main house for tea and after wards managed enough energy for a couple of beers before heading home to their respective beds. The work went on in the same vein all that week until all the houses and also the main house was stocked to capacity with the cords of lumber for the fires, they also stocked up two of the sheds of empty houses as well and built a second timber shed at the back of the main house beside the other existing shed as they went through more timber there than anywhere else. By the end of the week their muscles had become used to what they were doing and there were hardly any complaints from the men although that was more because the women had been giving them a hard time and calling them wimps than any other reason.

The following week Mary asked was there any chance that they could slaughter a couple of the livestock for food and to stock up the freezers that were empty of meat.

The next day a party of the men went up to the farm armed with some butchers knives and hatchets and a couple of books on butchery and cutting of meat into the different cuts that they had acquired for just such an occasion so as not just to hack it apart. They decide to start with one of the pigs first. It was shot in the head and brought into a shed that had been erected up at the farm for storing animal feed

They already had a large solid bench in the shed for butchering the animals on.

They managed to split the pig into two from nose to tail and then started following the directions for cutting up the carcase into the different cuts of meat. After a couple of hours they had managed to butcher the pig reasonably successfully and packed it all into three large plastic bins for transport back to the house. It was decided to try the sheep next so first of all it was decided to shear the animal and then slaughter it. This was duly done not without a great deal of difficulty because it was the first time they had tried to cut the wool off a sheep. Eventually the animal was killed and they proceeded to cut up the animal into the different cuts of meat and found that they had to cut the meat differently from what they had done with the pig. By the time they were finished and had again packed the meat into plastic bins they were all tired and covered in blood, someone remarked I now know where the term covered in blood like a slaughter house comes from. They decided to call it a day and bring what they had done back to the house and get washed up and they would read the books on slaughtering cattle that night and tackle it the next day. They returned to the house and carried their bins of meat into the house and under Mary's supervision they labelled and packed it all away in the freezers. They then headed for showers to try and get cleaned up.

That night they all had pork steaks for tea and all agreed it was worth all the hard work involved. Mary brought them down to earth and said she was glad to hear that and maybe the experience would make their task a lot easier the next day when they were slaughtering the cow. Someone spoke up and said they were not killing a cow tomorrow but a bullock, one of the children spoke up and said they would never eat meat again after what they had seen today.

That night everyone went to bed feeling very satisfied with their progress as a community and it was remarked that in some ways they had it better than before the death and all they were missing out on were the bad things and things that they could do without such as pornography and TV and pollution from all the cars and factories.

That immediately started a debate about TV and everyone had favourite programmes that they said they missed. Anne spoke up and said her grand mother used to say that the TV turned the family circle into a semi circle and families had lost the art of conversation and just being families. After a lazy evening that some passed playing cards or table games with the children although some of the adults were worse than the children when it got down to arguing about the rules and were caught cheating that of course they vehemently denied doing.

The next day they headed back up to the farm to the butchery shed. A large tarpaulin was put down on the ground and they tried to manoeuvre the bullock on to. This took ages as the animal could smell all the blood from the previous day and plain refused to be manoeuvred so that they just had to get it as close as possible before someone was hurt and had a foot broken when the animal stood on someone for about the fifth time and tried to butt everyone at the same time. Eventually with six men lifting the animal they managed to get it onto the tarp and started off disembowelling it and cleaning out its insides and hosing it down and then cutting off its legs and cutting them up first into the cuts of meat indicated in the book and then cutting the main carcase into two sections from nose to tail. They decided that for the future they would have to get a pulley and hooks hung from the ceiling before trying to slaughter an animal again as they could see it would make their job so much easier. By three that afternoon they had managed to finish the job after taking an hour and a half for lunch and had again packed all the meat into five bins and transported it all back to the house. There was more than enough to fill the large chest freezer they had for the beef only so it was decided that all the separate houses could have some fresh meat to put into their separate freezers which would make it handy for them because it meant that they would not have to come up to the house every time they wanted a cut of beef for a roast or a steak to put in the pan. Mary then turned round and told them not to think they were finished yet as she wanted some fowl to put into the freezer and that the next day they could go up to the farm and get a half a dozen hens or cocks that the girls would point out as the ones that were not laying and would be replaced by the young chickens that they had coming on and she expected that when they reached her kitchen there would not be a feather to be seen. So the next morning a couple of the men accompanied by the three children went back up to the farm and managed to catch after a wild scattering match from the hens the indicated six fowl made up of three cocks and three hens. They were duly presented to Mary minus their feathers but not cleaned out. The fowl were cleaned and frozen and packed away for use in the future.

The next item on the agenda for the village was to get in feed for the animals to last them for the winter. They needed oats, meal and dried cattle cakes as well as hay. Over the next week they went out to a couple of meadows near by and cut the long grass and left it to dry in the summer sun for the best part of a week until it had dried out then they went out and stacked the hay into stooks and let the sun finish off the process of drying the hay completely so that it could then be gathered and put into bales and brought back to the farm sheds and packed away. They decided that their hard work had produced enough hay to last the animals for the winter months and now they had to find a farm produce merchant and get together the oats and meal and cattle cakes. They sent out the two double axle trucks for this task and Bobbie and Joseph went in one truck and Jason and Don went in the other one.

They decided to head for Norwich as one of the nearest sizeable towns that was not to far away and according to the local telephone directory had two feed merchants in the town. After a trip that was hassle free other than negotiating the potholes that were becoming more frequent and the branches of trees that had to be removed the trip was uneventful, when they entered the town they went straight to the closest feed merchant. The premises had large double gates across a driveway up the side of a large shed and had the usual shop front on to the street that obviously contained their offices. They had brought a pair of bolt cutters with them so the padlocked gates presented no problems to them. They backed the two trucks up the driveway that was up the side of the shed. Again the bolt cutters came into play in getting access to the shed through its huge double doors that led on to the lane. When they went inside they found everything that they wanted. There were bales of hay that despite the time since they had been cut were in quite good condition but they left them alone and loaded some bales of straw, and sacks of oats and meal and also found cattle cakes and licks that they loaded as well. Also loaded on to the trucks were some new saddles, reins, stirrups, blankets and waterproof horse coats, a hand plough and the traces required for it and the harnesses and reins needed for a horse to pull a cart, also something that no one had thought of were chicken pellets and a couple of self feeding dishes and water dishes for the hens. After a discussion they decided to go and find another truck and to load it up with more straw and a variety of bags of food for all the animals. While they were out hunting for the truck which did not take them too long to find they also went looking for flood lights to mount along the top of the boundary fencing and sheets of corrugated iron that they were going to nail on the outside of the panels of fencing up to the height of six feet so that when the rats came in over the snow in the winter they would not be able to gnaw their way in through the timber fencing because it would be faced with the sheets of iron.

They reckoned that they would have to make at least another couple of runs to gather enough of the sheets of iron to complete the job.

It was decided to head home and off load what they had gathered and to return the next day for more iron sheets. They returned home bit quicker than their outward trip because they had cleared the road on that trip, but care still had to be taken because of the size of some of the pot holes that would easily break an axle.

They entered the village before darkness had fallen and off loaded their loads at the different areas that they were to be stored at. And everyone in the village came to give a hand to put everything away. John mentioned that he thought it was a good idea to acquire the third truck to help cut down the number of runs required backwards and forwards. After everything was put away in its place they all set off for the main house and relaxed while waiting for their tea. The next morning they set off again with the three trucks only this time they had Peter Woods and his partner Jean in the third truck. They all headed straight for the supply of sheet iron that they had found the previous day and started loading it on to the trucks. It was heavy work and they soon tired and decided to have a break and the flasks of coffee weer opened and they all relaxed for a short time. When the recommenced they worked at the task until all three trucks were full to capacity. Then after a side trip to the towns largest butchery to load up a cutting block, pulleys, chains, hooks, and more knives they then headed back home.

When they arrived they found that practically everyone was already out on the fence line putting up the sheets of iron that they had brought back the previous day. They were asked.

"What kept you so long we have been waiting for you since ten o clock this morning when we finished putting up the last lot?"

"Bullshit", came back the answer just as quickly. As they started unloading the first truck where they said they wanted it and then unloaded the other two trucks where indicated. They found that the team putting up the panelling had also put extra mesh on the two security gates and along the parapets of the bridge where the gates were mounted on either side. They then asked the fencing team.

"What have you not finished the first two truck loads that we unloaded yet? God but you are slow."

They barely escaped with their lives from the clods of earth that were showered at them. They dropped off the butchery equipment at the butchers shed at the farm and then made their way back into the village to relax with a beer in front of the fire that was always kept lit in the lounge at the main house even though it was summer and not required, it was just that everyone liked the fire lit and the homely atmosphere that it created. The next day they did the same thing all over again and found that they had eight sheets of iron left over and they could be used as roofing for the guard posts up on top of the fencing line.

Over the next couple of weeks they directed all of their efforts in trying to make the fence line around the village as secure as they could make it. They also refined the slaughter shed and made it a bit more hygienic as well and mounted the pulleys securely to the rafter beams and stored all the butchery items in the shed including the plastic boxes for packing and carrying the meat back to the house. The children had taken the task upon themselves to oil all the leather work on the saddles, reins and stirrup leathers for the horses and to hang everything up neat and tidy where any vermin would not be able to reach them. All the sheds were made as waterproof as was possible and the byres and horse stalls were made more comfortable for the animals.

They still made trips into the local towns and villages and brought back as many supplies as they could manage including stockpiling the supply of petrol in jerry cans.

One of the women said it would be a good idea if they brought back a supply of toys for presents for the children's birthdays and Christmas morning and hid them away so that they could have some pleasant surprises as they all worked very hard and did not have to be told to do anything, their chores were done without complaint whatever the weather brought that particular morning. So it was arranged that a couple of the women would accompany the next trip into Kings Lynn because it had a large toyshop in it.

The Summer progressed into autumn and John and a couple of the men even found time to do a bit of fishing in the Graven for brown trout and managed to catch quite a few, so that there were even some left over for freezing even with them being eaten nearly as quick as they were caught. It was decided that everyone in the village would be divided into two halves and they would make two trips into two different near by towns and let everyone do a bit of personal shopping in the line of clothes or whatever they wanted before winter set in with a change of weather. They would take six vehicles each trip so as to give everyone a bit more freedom and not have to keep waiting on everyone to finish what they were doing before moving on to the next shop. They would go fully armed and the men would keep watch over the women as much as possible because they reckoned they would finish shopping first.

This thought received a few cat calls from the ladies. The first trip set off in a holiday atmosphere and everything was accomplished without any problems. The second trip again had a holiday atmosphere like a day trip to the sea side, they even had a picnic lunch brought with them. Again there were no major incident other than shooting a couple of dogs that got a bit too close for comfort and also a few rats.

The radio was still not giving them any joy although it was tried every evening by going through the wave bands. They had reckoned from the numbers in their group and the area they had been spread over that only approximately one person in every half million had survived the five day sickness as they had started calling it. So that meant that really there were only about one hundred and twenty to one hundred and thirty people left in the whole of great Britain as the population for 2009 was just over sixty one million. This meant that they as a group were probably one of the largest groups in the country if not the largest group and this would help account for the poor results with the radio.

The next thing anyone knew was that the first winter frosts arrived and people started dressing in heavier clothes and soups started to appear on the menu at lunch and tea time and were gratefully received. November arrived and still there were frosts but thank goodness still no snow but the weather each day looked more like it every morning when they got up and that was a problem in itself, the getting up bit, into a cold bedroom. You always knew when winter had arrived because you started taking your under clothes into bed with you under the covers so as to give them some heat before you climbed into them and faced the cold bedroom and bathroom.

John and Anne along with just about everyone else headed to the main house for breakfast and the long suffering Mary who still cooked for everyone along with Rosemary's help and wouldn't hear of anyone else taking over the chore of preparing three meals a day for nearly the entire village.

John thought that the reason that everyone headed for meals over to the main house was mainly the companionship and security from the thought of an empty world where everything they had grown up with was gone for ever and possibly it would take another two hundred years or more before any semblance of the past occurred again, things like going to an office to work, holidays, cruise ships aeroplanes for travelling from A to B, catching a train, travel around the world and all the other things we took for granted. At least the worlds climate has a chance to recover and the ozone layer to repair itself with no more factory chimneys belching out smoke and harmful chemicals.

CHAPTER 9

THE SECOND WINTER.

After breakfast was over a general discussion ensued and they started making out the inevitable list of items that they thought were needed before the snow arrived and cut them off from going outside the village. Also Rusty brought up a point for discussion that no one had given much thought to.

"I am a bit worried about our cache of petrol cans at the far end of the village. I know nobody in the village smokes or would go near the petrol dump with a naked flame but we have all heard of Murphy's law and the fact that it never lets you down, there must be all of three hundred jerry cans down there and if they went up it has the potential to practically take the village with it, I would like to suggest that without any delay we split the dump into four separate places, well scattered so we can never have a chain reaction effect if anything did happen."

Several of the women present were immediately concerned with the thought of the possibility. After a further discussion everyone agreed that Rusty had a valid point and they should immediately start to split up the dump into sections of no more than one hundred cans each. Having decided to take action they immediately headed out the door and down the street to the petrol dump and on the way they decided where to put the different caches, also it was decided that they should put a roof over the top of the cans to keep the summer sun from overheating the metal cans. Several of the men went off to gather up the necessary lumber and sheet iron for the proposed roofs before they moved the petrol. It took them four days to erect the necessary protection for the cans of petrol from the weather especially the summer sun that had been known to climb to forty two degrees in the past. The dumps were well spread out and away from any of the residential houses as much as they could and then the cans were moved into their respective caches. They found when they counted that they had three hundred and eighty three cans of ten gallons each. They built four separate dumps and those along with the existing dump gave them the capacity to store five hundred cans of petrol, that meant that they needed to gather up an additional one hundred and seventeen additional cans and then they would call it quits on that particular aspect of their scavenging. They moved all the cans to their respective dumps and by the end of the week everything was in place and everyone heaved a sigh of relief. The men were just glad to get the job over and done with and the women seemed more relieved from the safety aspect, but all agreed that it was a job well done and a necessary one at that.

They continued putting together the last list before the snow arrived, needless to say one of the items on the list were the remaining one hundred and seventeen cans for petrol. The ground underfoot in the mornings was definitely crunchy from the frost from the night before. The calendar had moved on to the twentieth of November, as time waited for no one. So on the following Tuesday morning at eight o'clock three vehicles left the compound, one range rover, one double axle and one panel van with two people in each vehicle. The flat bed double axle went off to Cambridge to see if they could find any more of the ten gallon jerry cans as they knew they had cleaned out their immediate area. The other two vehicles headed for Kings Lynn to raid the supermarkets and other shops with their lists of goods required. One of the items on their list were Christmas decorations, enough for all the separate residences as by mutual consent it had been decided that they would make a real effort to regain the spirit of Christmas not only for the children's sake but everyone seemed to need it and want it. By the end of the day when someone looked at their watch they saw it was just after three o'clock and decided to call it quits except if anyone wanted to get anything special out of any of the shops for a present. It was just after four o'clock when they drove out of Kings Lynn and headed home. It was remarked that the dog packs had left them alone for a change and even the rats had kept their distance even though their numbers did not seem to have decreased any.

They arrived back to the village as dusk fell with its winter suddenness, when they arrived back they saw that the other truck had beaten them to it and were busy unloading the petrol they had acquired on their trip. When asked how they had got on they replied that they had managed to get seventy cans and that was definitely the last of jerry cans to be had in Cambridge and they were going to have to look elsewhere for the remaining forty seven cans required to fill their quota.

As usual when a scavenging party returned the complete population of the village turned out to give a hand to unload the trucks and pack away all the goods brought back. The Christmas decorations were split up between the different houses and a couple of spare boxes were put away for any one in the future who moved into their own residences.

As usual Mary and Rosemary had prepared a lovely meal for the returning party and for everyone else who wanted to eat in the main house. There was home made pumpkin soup, home grown vegetables and roast beef along with again home made horseradish sauce and to finish she had made a marmalade cake and fresh cream from their own cows. They also opened several bottles of wine to help the meal go down.

They decided to go out again the next morning in two vehicles, one panel van and one double axle flat bed truck that they would hopefully use to bring back the petrol. provided they could come up with the cans required for the storage of it. It was decided to try Holt and Kings Lynn for the jerry cans as they did not think they had stripped those places clean yet. Holt was only able to come up with twenty-four can's which were filled immediately. They drove on to Kings Lynn and after their sixth call they managed to fill their self imposed quota of another twenty three cans to bring them up to the required forty seven.

It was decided at the meeting held on the first of December that they would stop the school work for the girls until the end of January and they would send out another expedition after the snow had all gone, this time they would visit Ipswich, London and go further south to Woking and possibly Southampton. The trip would probably last three to four weeks as the round trip was probably about four hundred miles so they decided that they would make it a party of four in two vehicles.

There was an agreement made that they did not require any more food or any other items for the storage rooms until after the snow had come and gone as they felt they were pretty well organised for the winter hibernation as some one named the expected snow fall and the circumstances following which forced them to stay within the village perimeter. The only ones who seemed to be doing any work was the farm contingent which included Bobbie and the three girls and Mary and Rosemary with them still doing the cooking for anyone who turned up at the main house at meal times and that was most of the village. Everyone just seemed contented and felt secure in the main house with everyone around them.

A routine became established that after breakfast Mary was asked what chores anyone could help her with and she divided out tasks which included washing and peeling potatoes or other root vegetables, churning the milk to make butter or cheese, bring in firewood take out any rubbish and generally tidy up the house. Other than that it was not too hard to find someone who would like to play a game of monopoly or play a game of cards using counters for money as money as such no longer had any value as everything in the village was treated as communal property and it seemed to suit everyone.

The first snowfall occurred on the eleventh of December, during the night and as sometimes happens when it snows the temperatures seemed to rise rather than fall. So it was a pleasant day and everyone went outside and threw snowballs at each other and they made the inevitable snow man that the children loved. A large pine tree was found and cut down and brought into the lounge in the main house and decorated with the baubles and streamers of tinsel and some balloons and also streamers were hung from the ceiling from one corner of the room to the other.

Time went slowly by and the next thing it was Christmas eve and the children were told to hang their stocking from the mantle shelf over the fire place, which they delightedly did, Rosemary was told she still was not too old for Father Christmas to visit and she was to put her stocking up too, she did so to much good hearted cat calling which got worse when it was discovered that someone had substituted a huge stocking for Rosemary's and put her name on it and no matter how much she explained it was not her stocking and she had not put it out she was told by everyone that they did not believe her. Presents all wrapped up in shiny foil paper and with large bows on them started to appear under the tree as time went by and everyone was told they were not allowed to examine them until Christmas morning.

Christmas morning dawned and everyone in the village arrived at the house early to be greeted by John with a huge plastic bucket of egg nog that everyone applied themselves to liberally. The children took down their stocking and amid squeals of delight started to unpack the goodies from them and everyone else descended on the tree and found presents underneath it for everyone. Mary after her second glass of egg nog said she would have to get on with the lunch or she would be too tipsy to make it and they would all starve.

Eventually Christmas lunch was served with the tunes of Christmas Carols played on one of the girls CD players. It had all the goodies that one expected at Christmas. Egg nog, Roast chickens as they had not been able to find any turkeys anywhere, brussel sprouts, peas, cauliflower and white sauce, mashed and roast potatoes, mince pies, Christmas pudding liberally dowsed in brandy, and custard and fresh cream and even some ice cream was made with the snow arriving just in time to help freeze it. To finish off the meal there was Christmas cake for those that could fit it in and liqueurs and of course there was a plentiful supply of red and white wine served along with the main course and there was the inevitable coffee for the addicts. Up to Christmas the snow had confined itself to light falls and flurries but no large falls. After Christmas and the New Year arrived so did the snow with a vengeance, On the third of January there was a very heavy fall of snow during the night and it continued all of the next day as well. It was decided at the village meeting at the first of the month that at the first sign of heavy snow they would step up the patrols along the fence line to keep a special look out for any rats starting to gather in numbers. They had already installed the extra flood lights along the top of the fencing right around the entire perimeter. It was agreed that one of the weak parts of their defence were the two gates at either end of the village and if one was to use shotguns there they would have to be careful that the blasts from the shotguns did not do more harm than good by cutting the wire mesh with the pellets, so it was decided to have two people at either end of the village at the gates to have the use of flame throwers they had brought back with them from the armoury, four of the weapons and several back up canisters of the plasma for them, so it was agreed to place two at either end and also to place jerry cans of petrol along the river bank that could be poured into the river and being petrol it would float on the surface and if they set it alight the floating petrol may help provide a defence against the rats.

Over the next few days the rat numbers were seen to be gathering completely around the village. At the fencing line they had an added but not thought of bonus with the sheets of corrugated iron they had put up on to the fencing in that the bottom of the sheets of iron were resting on the wire mesh which allowed the electric current to travel from the wire mesh on to the sheets of iron and when the rats walked across the snow over the wire mesh with immunity, the minute they touched the corrugated iron they were immediately electrocuted and fried to crispy critters with the amount of power from the generators being pumped into the electrification system. The fencing looked as if it was completely successful as a deterrent against the rats or any other predator and may not have to be defended at all so they could concentrate on the gates and the river. By the end of a week of heavy snow the rats were to be seen gathering on the far river bank in their thousands, if not millions and everyone was becoming very nervous. Both men and women were out on patrol and everyone was ready if the rats looked like they were going to attack, every one wore long legged thick boots that were hoped would offer their lower legs some protection against a bite and thick gloves and wrist bands. After a week of sleepless nights with the snow never letting up for very long and the opposite river bank getting closer because of the heavy snow drifts along both sides of the river banks extending out into the river until the gap in the middle was only about four feet wide.

Suddenly as if on a signal the rats at both ends of the village at the gates were attacking in force and trying by sheer weight of numbers to force their way through and building a mound of electrified bodies up against the gates that they could climb and leap over the top of the gates. The flame throwers were then turned on at that stage and even though it was virtually impossible to see anything through the smoke and flames from the jets of plasma directed at the rats it seemed to be working in that the rats were obviously becoming more reluctant to face the burning jelly like substance shot out of the nozzles of the flame throwers and had stopped trying to rush the gates and were just milling around in confused terror. At the same time this was happening the rats along the opposite river bank had stopped running back and forth and suddenly all seemed to rush towards the river together and threw themselves into the running water in such numbers that even though some of the first wave of rats had been swept away by the river there were suddenly so many bodies in the water that the next tide of rats were able literally able to run across the gap in the river using the backs of their comrades already in the water.

Someone shouted out in terror "For God's sake would someone pour the bloody petrol into the water and set it on fire before we are over run." The first wave of rats had reached the village side to the river and were making their way over the hard caked snow and ice and were trying to climb the frozen snow covered muddy banks and every one was blasting at them with shotguns and it could be seen that the rats were starting to win the engagement the more they got reinforcements over the running water at the centre of the river. The electric generators had not been fired up as yet because of the people standing on top of the mesh fighting the rats with their shotguns.

At last the petrol was poured into the river at several points along the bank and was set alight with a whoosh of flames at four different points. The flames soon started to travel along the river having been taken by the flow of water and the flames were three and four feet high in places and they kept adding to the continuos river of fire that now covered the length of the river by adding more and more petrol, so that the river of fire now extended beyond the village fencing line on the down side of the river. John called out to everyone.

"Stop pouring petrol." As he could see that the rats had stopped trying to cross the river. So they stopped pouring petrol onto the river and concentrated firing at the rats with shotgun fire at those still alive on their side of the river that had made the crossing and were scrabbling around without any seeming direction or were trying to climb the river bank at their side.

"We beat them off that time but I think they will try again before the night is over!" Said John to his companions. "Did many get past us and into the village."

"Not to many that I could see in the heat of the attack." Replied Rusty from up the defence line a bit and everyone else seemed to agree that there had not been more than a dozen or so had managed to get past them and make a run of it into the village itself.

Jason spoke up. "I saw both Max and Jessie chasing some of them and they had managed to dispatch a few between them and they were still off chasing after the survivors, so I would worry more about the next attack rather than what got past us."

A few of the women went back to the house in the lull of fighting and collected flasks of soup that the girls had been making for them so as to put some heat back into their bones, because now that the battle was over and the adrenalin had stopped flowing everyone was suddenly starting to feel the cold a bit.

They also took the time to restock the piles of empty jerry cans with full ones ready for the next onslaught. At either ends of the village the gates were eased open and the piles of dead rats were shovelled into the river or to one side so as not to give the expected next rush of rats an advantage by using them as jumping off points in the next attack that everyone was expecting because there still seemed to be millions of rats gathered in the fields across from them and milling around and squeaking their anger at the humans who had dared to defy them.

Suddenly a shout went up. "Here they come." Again the rats seemed to be using the technique that they had found worked for them the last time using the first couple of waves to fill the gap between the banks with bodies that they could use as a bridge to run over, although the petrol burning in the river the last time had made the gap wider that they had to span so it took a lot more bodies to bridge the gap but they managed but by that time the petrol was already being poured into the river, the defenders had also learned and had started pouring petrol sooner, in fact they started the minute the charge had commenced from the other bank. The minute the petrol was lit it seemed that an instantaneous wall of flame had sprung up the full length of the river fronting the village. Amidst the flames and smoke all that could be heard were the squeals of the rats as they burned to death either mid river or as they continued to burn when they reached the village river bank or when they turned back and set some of the milling hordes on the opposite river bank on fire as they ran amongst them in terror trying to get away from their petrol soaked fur that was afire and consuming them as it was fanned by the wind created by themselves as they ran but to no avail as there was no escaping the flames once they had caught hold.

The second attack was beaten off it was thought quicker than the first one and then it was a matter of again finishing off with the shotguns those rats that were milling about at the waters edge on their side of the river bank, it was thought that this time none had gained the top of the river bank to escape into the village. After their second defeat the rats seemed to move off out of sight into the fields beyond the river and there were no more attacks that night and other than a well manned patrol everyone else managed to grab some much needed sleep. The next morning everyone had a get warm breakfast and then relieved the night patrol and they returned to the main house to have a well earned breakfast and then to collapse into their respective beds so as to be ready for the next night.

During the day again people went to the two gates and shovelled the bodies of the rats back from the vicinity of the gates so that the rats could not use them to their advantage and the defences were examined in detail and the wire mesh strengthened if anyone had any doubts about any of it although it all looked in good order and the wire connections for the generators to the gates was also examined in detail to make sure it was all in good working order. Satisfied that the gates were ready for the next onslaught they all moved to the river bank except for the roving patrols that were keeping a watchful eye on the enemy that could be seen in the distance milling about, they climbed down to the edge of the river and shovelled the dead rats that were on their side of the bank into the middle of the river and broke away any snow drifts that were still clinging to the river bank and thus narrowing the river width. This meant that the rats were going to have to use more bodies to try and bridge the river at any point that they choose as a crossing point. In hindsight this should have been done at the start of the heavy snow and during the snow falls to stop that happening but no one had for a minute thought that the rats would be cleaver enough to think of that method of trying to gain access to the village, no one would underestimate the rats again and that was for sure.

Nothing happened for the next three nights and then on the fourth nigh it had started to snow and visibility was not good , when one of the lookouts sounded the alarm as the rats were trying the same tactics using the cover of the snow fall to help mask what they were doing. They were having a more difficult time bridging the gap between both sides of the river because of the gap being widened by the defenders over the last few days on not only their side of the river but on the opposite river bank as well. The petrol was poured into the river and set afire immediately and again the rats were consumed by the hungry flames. The attempts on the gates at either end of the village was only a half hearted attempt and was thought to be more of a diversion rather than a proper attempt. The attempt on the river was beaten off with out any of the potential invaders gaining a foothold on their side of the river bank, there was only the one attempt that night.

Everything quietened down after that last attempt and although the rats could still be seen across the river there did not seem to be the same numbers. By the end of January they seemed to over the worst of the snow and there were just a few falls of snow and the usual frost before it disappeared again for another year.

They had used a total of fifty one cans of petrol beating off the attacks of the rats and seven cylinders of the flame throwers jelly like plasma and it was decided that the first thing to be done as well as the usual scavenging for food and what ever else that had been put onto the usual lists was to replace the emptied cans of petrol, and flame throwers plasma they would need to build ups about five stocks of petrol cans along the river bank in addition to the existing stockpile of jerry cans.

All the empty jerry cans were loaded onto one of the flat bed trucks and an expedition was mounted to refill their expended petrol resources and gather together the required extra cans needed and to replace the flame throwers jelly cylinders and replace the shotgun cartridges used up. As well as that the two panel vans were dispatched to restock the food that had been used over the winter months. Over the next week the foraging trips proved to be successful and everything on their lists were found and brought back to the village.

The next thing it was decided to do was to get people with spades and shovels to make the river banks steeper on both sides of the river bank and to get rid of any flat areas so that both sides of the river the banks came down steeply to the waters edge and it was hoped that this would help make the task of crossing the river more complex for the rats for the next winter also the wire mesh from the top of the river bank was dismounted and remounted down the side of the river bank itself to see if that worked better, it also left the top of the river bank on the village side a flatter area for the defenders to have a more secure footing for themselves. By the end of February all these jobs had been accomplished and it was decided to plan the next expedition that they had talked about before the winter had set in.

The next items of good news that were announced at dinner one night were that not only Brian and Joanne were going to be parents but so also were Hal and Alice. There was great celebration at the announcement of the news as it made everyone feel that at last they would have a future. The girls were told that this was going to be their last evening drinking alcohol so make the most of it but not to indulge too much. Over the next few day the prospective parents were showered with gifts and wool and knitting needles suddenly appeared on the next shopping lists on the kitchen wall. Brian started into making a couple of baby cribs one for himself and Joanne and also the other for Hal and Alice.

Any rats that had made it into the village the two dogs plus the family of cats seemed to have made short work of along with the rat traps that were scattered about the village and were inspected on a regular basis.

It was finally decided that John and Anne would head up the expedition and Rusty would be left in charge of the village as usual and that Mike and his partner Beth, would accompany John and Anne, they decide that as discussed before Christmas that the areas that they would cover would be first to Ipswich then on to London and spend a bit of time in London and then to Woking and finish up at Southampton and then work their way back. At first it had been suggested that the round trip would take three weeks but this was changed to a four week trip because the roads were getting a lot worse and it may just take them a lot longer on the outward trip because of that. Two of the Range Rovers were serviced as best as they could do and stocked up with petrol and two spare jerry cans were loaded on to the roof racks of each along with a couple of spades, crow bars, towing wires, a small acetylene torch kit and its small bottles of oxygen and acetylene, chain saws, tents sleeping bags, water, food and torches along with spare batteries. Anything that they had forgotten to pack they reckoned they could scavenge along the way. Just as they were getting ready to wave good bye Hal appeared running and waving a bag with some emergency medical supplies in it that they were told with a smile to bring back unopened. So they set off on their longest trip of exploration that they had made so far since the great death had struck down the worlds population.

CHAPTER 10

THE TRIP OF EXPLORATION.

They set off at ten past eight that morning and made quite good time until they reached Cambridge because the had cleared the road on their previous trips and there were not to many obstacles along the way to slow them down.

From Cambridge to London the roads were starting to revert to nature in a big way with the usual pot holes, but the most surprising thing were the size of the trees that had started to grow in the middle of the roads plus the usual trees that had fallen across the roads and were either blocking or partially blocking them and they had no choice but to cut them up with the chain saws and then lever the cut logs to the road side, this seemed to take a long time and they still had not reached London before they were forced to call a halt for the night and find shelter in a house along the road side. So far they had not met any large packs of dogs or rats for that matter, but they still took no chances and made sure the house they were staying in was secure before they settled down for the night after a feed cooked on a mentholated spirit stove that they had brought with them. Eventually they settled down in one room in front of a fire that they lit to help keep out the winter chill that was still out there.

The next morning they set off on their way to London and except for the usual melody of pot holes and trees to keep them busy they reached the outskirts of London that evening and this time found a pub and settled in there for the night. Again in front of a log fire only this time they each had a glass of spirits to help keep them warm as well as the fire. They set of at seven in the morning after a hot drink and a couple of slices of toast made on the grill of the spirit stove and started to explore London. There was evidence of fires everywhere they looked, a couple had even wiped out whole streets before they had met some obstacle that had finally stopped them. By the end of the day they had seen no evidence of life anywhere they had looked. It was decided to call it a day and find somewhere to sleep. They found a small hotel and decided that it would do them for the night. The front door was unlocked and it was just a matter of opening the door and walking inside. They found a lounge bar with comfortable seats and lounge chairs in it. They made something to eat and settled down with a couple of drinks for the night after making sure that the doors were locked and that there were no livestock of any type who would dispute their residence during the night.

The next morning they set off again to explore London. There were heaps of skeletons lying around everywhere they looked either in vehicles or just lying in the road or on the pavement, there was even a bus full of skeletons sitting at the edge of the road, it looked as if the people on it did not even have the energy to get out of the bus before they succumbed to the illness, as if the driver had pulled in to the edge of the road and at a signal he and everyone on board had died. There were also lots of partial skeletons lying around that had obviously been dismembered by animals.

They decided to find a housing estate in one of the suburbs and then find a large supermarket and sit outside it and do the same as they had in Norfolk,. Fire off six shots with a count of five between each shot and then wait ten minutes and repeat the same pattern for an hour, if they do not get any results they would move location and try the same again in another area. They did not get any results so they moved on to another area and tried the same again.

By three in the afternoon they had stopped and tried they had stopped eight times and had no results in any of the areas except draw the attention of a pack of monkeys and also a couple of lions had come by in one area to see what was going on.

They decided to move on again and try one more area before they found somewhere to stay for the night, they drove for twenty minutes and then stopped and started firing again. After they had fired six patterns they heard a pattern of firing in reply. Excitedly they returned the fire pattern and continued to do so for another ten minutes when a car appeared at the top of the street and drove towards them. John stood up and placed his rifle down on the ground and his three companions deliberately got back into their vehicles. John stood in the middle of the road with his arms by his side and tried to give the impression of peaceful intentions. The vehicle came slowly forward and stopped about twenty feet away from their two vehicles, it could be seen that there were two persons inside. They both got out of the car and stood beside

e their car doors with rifles crooked in their arms.

John spoke to the two men. "Good afternoon gentlemen and he smiled at them, I am glad you heard our signals and decided to come and investigate. My companions and I are on a trip of exploration to see if there are many more people alive other than ourselves and our companions."

"My name is Peter and this is Luke, where are you from?" came back the reply.

"HI Peter my name is John and my companions are Anne." and he pointed to her. "This is Mike and his partner Beth and we come in peace, we mean you no harm as I said we are on a trip of exploration from where we have settled since the Death. Are there any more of you?"

"No there is just the two of us but we do know of another group in London of three, a man, a woman and a young boy. There was another man who had lived on his own but he had lost his mind and tried shooting anyone he saw and we had to finally shoot him ourselves before he killed us, we had already found a body of another man he had obviously killed."

"As I said we are on a trip, our next call was to be Woking and then on to Southampton before we returned home. We were just thinking of taking a break and having a cup of coffee would you like to join us?"

For the first time the other man Peter smiled and said we would love to join you for a cup of coffee and he started to walk forward and his companion was seen to get out of their vehicle, he also carried a rifle over his arm, he appeared to be in his late teens and the older man Peter appeared to be in his forties. Anne, Beth and Mike dismounted from their vehicles and Anne went round the back of their vehicle and pulled up the tail gate and removed the meth stove and what was needed to make coffee.

"Luke would you mind bringing our vehicle over here and place it in position." said Peter to his companion, who turned without a word and walked back to their car and drove it forward and parked it in such a manner as to make a third wall with his car and their two vehicles.
"I see from the look on your faces that you do not understand why we automatically do that, it is because of the wild animals and dog packs, it helps give us a measure of security. Do you not have any problems with dog packs where you are from?"

"Yes we do to a certain extent, but we have fortified where we live and they can not get into the village, so they are no longer a problem unless we go outside the village on a scavenging trip. We have had more trouble with the rats, they attacked us last winter in the millions and we only just managed to beat them off and defeat them."

"How many of you are there in your group?"

"At last count there were twenty four of us men women and children of all ages. We have managed to bring in everyone virtually in our part of southern

England and that is why we are doing a sweep now to see if there was anyone else alive in London and down to Southampton."

"Tell us a bit more about what you have managed to achieve?" asked Peter.

John looked at his companions who nodded to him so he gave a potted version of what had transpired with their group since the Death just over two years ago.

"My God but you seem to have managed to organise yourselves very well, we just moved into a posh hotel and searched London for any other survivors, that is how we found the other group of three over in the west end. Look you seem to be very well organised and I must say it is a bit lonely here on our own, would it be possible to join your group, I am a Doctor or should I say I was a Doctor and young Luke is healthy and can turn his hand to just about anything."

Anne who was watching and listening to the whole conversation intently and professed to be good at body language nodded her head at John and when he glanced at the other two they indicated that they would be happy to include them into the group.

John held out his hand to Peter and said "Welcome to our community." shook his hand and also Luke's hand, who smiled for the first time since they had met him.

"We will be keeping to our schedule, will you mind going along with us down to Southampton? It seems there is no reason to hang about in London to search anymore as you have already done so and there is no one else in the city other than the other small group, do you think they will want to join us as well or do you think they would prefer to be on their own?"

"Why don't I take you over to meet them and you can ask them yourself before you continue on your trip!" Replied Peter to John.

"Fine that sounds like a good idea." Remarked John.

Peter drove his car in front of the other two and took them over to the outskirts of the West End of London and stopped outside an apartment block and stopped in the middle of the street and alighted from their car and honked his car horn a couple of times. The party from Hunsworth got out of their vehicles too and stood beside them but left all their firearms inside the vehicles other than side arms. After Peter had honked his horn a couple more times a man appeared in a doorway of an apartment block opposite them and hailed them.

"Yes Peter who are your companions?"

"They are people from Norfolk area who have formed a community there and came to London in search of anyone else left alive after the sickness killed everyone off. Luke and myself have asked to join their group and we brought them over to meet you and to see if you wanted to come along as well."

John stepped forward and introduced himself and his party and explained why they were in London and where they were going next.

The man asked them to wait while he got his companions and spoke to them and he turned on his heel and went back inside. After about ten minutes he returned and had a woman with him and also a young boy of about ten years of age who hung back at the doorway while the man and woman came down the steps and walked over to them, as he came closer they could see that he was about thirty years of age and his companion was in her middle twenties. As he walked up to the party he was obviously alert for any trouble and as was his partner who was examining the group very closely.

Before he could speak Anne stepped forward and smiled at the woman but offered to shake hands with the man who accepted though he was obviously thrown by Anne's friendly smile and attitude.

"Hi my name is Anne and this is my partner John and these are two very good friends of ours Mike and Beth and as Peter has said we are down in London looking for survivors who may want to join us or may not, they may be happy enough to be on their own, there is no pressure to join us, it has to be completely your own decision made of your own free will. Would you like me to tell you about our village and what we have achieved?" Having said her piece she made the effort to sit down on the kerb and smiled again at the couple and waited for them to speak.

"Hi my name is Sarah and this is my partner Adam and the boy over in the doorway is Paul." It could be seen that she was starting to relax.

"Let us tell you about ourselves and that may help you to make up your minds, if you decided to join us the only thing that will be expected of you is to help work in the village for the good of everyone, there is no pressure put on you, everyone does what work suits them and their skills and generally mucks in to help everyone for the good of all, we have a mixed community of twenty four people men, women and children and we have even started to school the children. She then went on to explain in detail about their home in Norfolk, during the conversation the boy made his way over to the group and listened to what was being said. Anne concluded by saying obviously you would want to talk it over amongst the three of you, why don't we come back in the morning before we continue on with our trip and you can give us your answer then?"

She stood up and groaned and said my bones must be getting too old for hunkering down like that, I did not realise that I had so many bones that can ache all at once, as she rubbed her knees and hips.

The woman Sarah said. "Thanks for your offer we will see you then in the morning about what time?"

John replied. "About eight o clock if that is all right by you."

"That will be fine." replied both Sarah and Adam and they said good bye to Peter and Luke and turned and walked away back over to their doorway and went back inside after turning and waving from the doorway.

They returned to Peter and Luke's residence at their invitation to spend the night with them.

They had a meal prepared on a gas stove that Peter and Luke had obviously rigged up and was connected to a gas cylinder similar to that used by caravans. The apartment in the hotel was very comfortable and after eating and talking for a couple of hours about the village they finally decided to head to bed. Just as John and Anne were going into their bedroom Peter said with a twinkle in his eyes I suppose you will tell us sometime where the village is exactly. "Good night."

"He is no idiot is he?" asked John of Anne. "He obviously had realised that I had deliberately held back the address of where we have settled until I was completely sure of them."

Anne smiled in reply and said. "It does not seemed to have upset him too much, does it?"

"No I agree, they seem to be all right and should be an asset to the village, especially I think we are lucky to get Peter with him being a Doctor, it is a skill that we needed badly even with the experts that we do have. It seems that young Luke was serving his time to be a carpenter he was in his final year so he should be handy to work with Brian. Do you think the others will join us?"

"I think it may be touch and go as to whether they will or not, having to look after the young boy may tip them over to coming with us, we will see."

The next morning they all packed up their gear and their hosts packed their car with what they wanted to take with them, which seemed to be mainly clothes and books which were mixed medical and novels. John explained about the reason they drove Range Rovers and suggested that they might change their vehicle if they were not too attached it. Peter agreed that it sounded a good idea and said if they would follow them he knew where the Rover Dealer was situated and he would do a swap. They followed him for about five miles and drew up outside a dealership and went inside and found what they wanted and after checking the oil and water and blowing up the tyres they swapped over their personal possessions into it and started off for the home of Sara, Adam and Paul and arrived a bit late at eight fifteen.

As they drew up at the door the three of them came down the steps and it was obvious that they had been waiting for them.

"Sorry we are a bit late." called out John, as you can see we had a bit of shopping to do and he indicated the new Range Rover being driven by Peter.

"That's okay." Said Adam with a smile we were beginning to think you had changed your minds with your offer.

"Lord no." spoke up Anne "I really am sorry to be late, things just took a bit longer than we thought they would, are you going to come with us?"

"Yes we would love to, it will be good to see other faces after the last couple of years."

"If after you have been with our community for how ever long it might be if you ever want to leave us we will send you on your way with our blessing and enough supplies and weapons that should help get you started again where ever you may want to go to. Do you have transport? Or would you like us to go and get you a vehicle like ours which is good for travel on the roads outside of town."

"Yes we do have transport but a vehicle like yours probably would be a good idea, if you don't mind."

No problem said Peter. "Luke and I will go and get you one." He looked over at John for his agreement and he nodded and smiled and said.

"Thanks Peter that would be a big help." The two new recruits drove off on their chore.

"Do you have much gear that you are bringing with you?" Queried John.

"No not a great deal mostly clothes and a few books and bits and pieces. They are all in a pile at the front door and Sarah is upstairs checking to see if we have forgotten anything"

It took an hour before Peter and Luke returned with the new vehicle for the latest recruits about to join the village community.

"It is fully checked over and full of petrol and we found a couple of jerry cans that we filled as well." Said Peter as he alighted from the vehicle and indicated a couple of jerry cans up on top of the roof rack.

"Marvellous, if you can give Adam and Sarah a hand to load their personal; possessions we will be on our way." Remarked John as he hefted a bundle of gear from the front door step where it had been piled ready to load into the vehicle and carried it over to the Rover and piled it into the back of the vehicle behind the rear seats in the luggage compartment. When everything was loaded they set off in a convoy of four vehicles on their way to Woking.

When they arrived at Woking they stopped in the main street in a defensive square formation with a vehicle on each of four sides which helped to give them added protection in the event of an attack by any wild animals. While the three ladies made lunch John did his usual stunt with his rifle firing off a round every five seconds for a total of six rounds then a five minute break before repeating the procedure, this was continued for one hour before they called a halt and decided that there was no one in the town or no one who wanted to make themselves known. They set off for Southampton after lunch without exploring Woking any further.

For some reason the roads seemed to deteriorate when they left the town, between potholes and trees and shrubs it made the going quite difficult, they were constantly in and out of the vehicles with the chain saws cutting a path for the cars to make their way through. By four in the afternoon they had only progressed about ten miles and the difficulty showed no signs of easing off. They decide to look for somewhere to stop for the night. They had travelled about another mile down the road when they came upon a roadside pub and eatery and decided it would be ideal for their purposes. They parked in the car park adjacent to the front door and went inside to explore. By mutual consent the ladies were always left outside when the men explored so they could remove any skeletons or any other grisly sights that might be lying around or possibly to evict a wild animal that may have made the place its home. In this instance there were three mummified remains in the front lounge bar and a couple of skeletal remains upstairs that were carried out the back door and were stacked like a cord of wood around the back out of sight.

The ladies were called inside and immediately headed for the kitchen to see what they could prepare in the way of a meal for everyone and the men headed for the bar and found some bottles of lager that matched their thirst from the day's hard work of clearing a path through the road blockages. The meal consisted of tiny taters that were tinned small potatoes and tasted great just like new potatoes, they also had tinned peas and tinned stewed meat and they found boxes of chocolate bars that had not gone off too badly and were quite edible, they had them for desert and opened several bottles of wine with the meal. The conversation that evening consisted off a question and answer session about the village that was going to be home for the five newcomers. The two ladies that were joining them seemed to be upset about the stories of the attacks by the rats and even the men were surprised about the numbers of rats that had attacked the village and the fact that they were so well organised. John and the others from the village did their best to reassure the newcomers that the village defences were sufficient to deter any future attacks.

They decide to call it a night at nine thirty and try for an early start in the morning.

The next morning Anne and the other women were up early at six and had breakfast ready in double quick time. It consisted of coffee and a couple of tinned pies that they heated in the kitchen oven's, they were run on bottled gas and proved great in heating the pies. They set off at seven thirty and had only travelled about half a mile when they had to dismount and cut up a large tree that had fallen across the road and had blocked it completely, after they had cleared the tree they got a good run before the next blockage which was a stream that was running across the road and they had to stop and explore its depth before driving across it in case there was a sudden fall off and damage an axel, it proved to be shallow it was only about six to eight inches deep.

The convoy continued towards Southampton and they reckoned they were over the half way mark by lunch time when they stopped for a bite to eat before tackling the last part of the journey. When they set off after lunch they made good time only having to stop three more times to remove obstacles from the road that were impeding their progress before they reached the outskirts of Southampton and drove down the London Road into the centre of the city and found themselves in the High Street and stopped outside a hotel called the De Vere Grand Hotel on the West Quay Road, that was also close to the dockland area.

They decide to call it a day there and again sorted out the hotel they had stopped outside and parked the vehicles in the forecourt outside the main entrance. They cleared any mummified remains from the lobby and the dining room and lounge bar. There were only about six bodies to remove to make the place look presentable.

They also cleared two double bedroom suites that had extra beds in them and a connecting door between the two of them and were on the first floor. After bringing in from their transport what they might need in the way of changes of clothes and firearms, they went back downstairs to explore and to find the kitchen and see what food there was available before having to go out and get some from one of the supermarkets. The larder in the kitchen was well stocked with tinned goods and also glass jars of pasta that appeared to be fresh, as usual the stoves and ovens were gas fired and in working order. The ladies were soon cooking up a storm and said that there was no need to go out to the supermarket to scavenge stores so the men as usual went in search of the lounge bar and soon helped themselves to whatever their taste dictated and they brought some bottles of Vodka split drinks in to the ladies in the kitchen to keep them going until they joined the men.

The food was served in the bar rather than the dining room and everyone ate and drank their fill. Then the front door was locked and they adjourned to the two bedrooms they had taken over and after making sure that the bedroom doors were locked and bolted and a heavy piece of furniture placed across the doors as an added precaution they all lay themselves down for what they hoped would be a good restful sleep. The next morning after breakfast they decided to send out two of the vehicles to see if they could attract any attention by the usual methods. The vehicle returned at four o clock in the afternoon with no results to their efforts. They went to bed after their usual precautions. The next morning another vehicle was sent out in a different direction to see how they would do and another two vehicles explored the Central Business District. There was a large supermarket just up the road and they went into it to see if any stock was missing off the shelves as that was usually a good indication of there being survivors in the area, they found that the stock was intact so they assumed there were no survivors in the immediate area.

The exploring vehicle returned with the same story. It was decided that they would send out one more Rover the next day and then they thought it was a safe bet to assume there was no one living in the city. Again the results were negative so they decided to explore up and down the coast for a short distance to see if they had any luck out of the city.

For another four days they explored the coastline in both directions but to no avail.

It was then decided to find a large panel or delivery van and to stock up on food and anything else that they thought may be useful to bring back with them as there were another five mouths to feed from now on and they did not want to deplete their stockpiles at the village and they thought that they should also stockpile some more clothes like jeans and woollen pullovers and anoraks, also boots and leggings.

They found a shop that sold overcoats and had a stock of Australian stockman's coats called Driza-bone and oiled hats that were guaranteed to keep out the wettest weather, so a plentiful supply of different sizes were added to the loot they had liberated.

John had a word with Peter about acquiring a range of surgical instruments, he explained that they had a fairly good supply of medicines and dressings etc but they had no surgical instruments and he thought it would be a good idea for them to go up to the hospital and raid the operating theatres for whatever he thought may be useful for any contingency in the future. Peter agreed that it was a very good idea and they should do it the next day as a priority.

The next day they went up to the hospital and gathered up a complete range of instruments and everything in triplicate and they also got a hold of some cylinders of oxygen and masks to administer it and some cylinders of anaesthetic gas and vials of anaesthetic and several boxes of different sizes of syringes. Also they acquired more antibiotics of different types in case the usual tried and true Penicillin did not work as had been happening with more frequency in the past. Peter thought as well that some boxes of plaster cast bandages were a good idea to have he also said when he saw the surgery they had at the village he would know more on what they were short of and required to get.

They had been away from home now for nearly three weeks and it was decided that as the delivery van they had acquired was full to bursting as well as the four Range Rovers they would start the return journey the next morning.

They headed back up the road they had used to come to Southampton and reached London before dark and decided to stop for the night at Adam and Sarah's old residence. They had a good meal that night and soon everyone was professing to be sleepy and they all decided by mutual consent to head for their beds. The next morning it was decided to have a general scout around London before heading back on to the road after lunch in case anything struck someone eye and they thought it would be a good idea to bring with them. Nothing occurred to anyone and they hit the road at twelve thirty. Because they had cleared the road on the way up to London there was no major difficulty encountered on the return journey by the convoy of four range rovers and the large delivery van. They decided to split their journey at the same place they had stopped on the way to London and return to the village the next morning. After a leisurely start in the morning they made their way home to the village and arrived in convoy at the bridge gate at eleven thirty. John pumped his horn twice and Rusty appeared out of the main house and came running up to the gate.

"Hi!. It is good to see you back, early is better than late, it means we don't have to worry about you. I see you have brought some more company back with you." As he spoke Rusty turned to the newcomers who had all alighted from their vehicles and war standing beside them and looking and a little lost and slightly awed with what they could see of the villages defences, because the eight foot high fence line stretched away from their left into the distance and the heavy mesh on the bridge gate. The next thing was that Max came bounding up to Anne and barking madly and Jessie was following along behind, he threw himself at Anne and reared up on to his hind legs to lick her face and then over to John who received the same greeting, he stopped then and looked at the new arrivals and John quickly spoke up. "This is Max and Jessie our dogs and very valuable members of our community, they would literally give their lives for any of you and Max has in the past saved Anne's life, so there is no reason to be afraid of them." He then brought Max over to each new member and introduced them, once the introductions to the dogs had taken place, John suggested they drive the vehicles down to the main house. "I will introduce everyone there." They drove the five vehicles down to the front of the main house and everyone started to arrive all at once. Introductions were made all round and John pulled a sheet of paper out of his pocket that he had been scribbling on. "I have here a list that I have made out for the allocations of sleeping quarters. I will ask Rosemary to bring you into the house and show you to your rooms. I am afraid it also means that some of you that already have rooms in the main house are going to have to shift around a bit to make things work out. Adam and Sarah if you would like to drive your vehicle down the road to the house with the yellow front gate that will be your house and you can unpack your Rover and move your gear inside and then if you come back to the house here we can unpack the salvage that is in your vehicle and Mary can load you up with food and anything else you require. All the salvaged goods always come here first so they can be added to one of our lists and packed away and then it can be given out to whoever needs it. Hal would you and Alice mind terribly if I asked you and Alice to move out of your house and move into the vacant house next door to you and I will move Peter Willkouby here who is one of our new arrivals and is a surgeon and a medical doctor into your house and he can then run the surgery and hospital with your help, also we have brought back a load of medical gear with us this trip."

"We won't mind in the least, actually Alice was just saying that she would like to see about moving into that cottage as it is slightly smaller and to use her words more quaint. Why don't you came with us Doctor and we will help you move in when we get our stuff moved out."

"Please call me Peter and not doctor that is too formal and I really hope you do not mind me taking over your house from you both." and he smiled at Alice as he spoke.

"No that is fine with us and welcome to our village." replied Alice and indicating that Peter follow them down the road to the house that they all called the surgery.

Young Paul was soon taken over from Rosemary by the three girls who immediately saw a new playmate and they made it their business to introduce him to his new bedroom and to help him move in his clothes and bits and pieces and of course everything was examined in minute detail if he had something that they didn't he was asked to explain how it worked, so the ice was soon broken and he lost his initial nervousness.

John went over to Mary and gave her a big hug and said. "I thought you didn't have enough to do lately so that is why I brought home some more people for you to cook for."

"You are terrible you great lummox, you know I don't mind and I see you have brought back with you a few supplies! The vehicles you bring back every trip are getting bigger and bigger yo will soon be arriving back with a great big twenty two wheel lorry next."

"I have not been able to find one yet, but I will try for the next trip just especially for you. Anne and I will go and unload our personal gear from the car and then we will see you at lunch, we are starving, we have not had a descent meal since we left here just over three weeks ago." He gave her another hug and Mary headed inside to continue with the preparations for lunch and to put more food on the menu for the extra mouths that had arrived. John and Anne went down the road with their vehicle and unloaded their personal clothes etc. and then walked back up the road to the main house and went inside to the pleasant atmosphere of the log fire burning in the lounge hearth and the smell of food cooking and coming from the kitchen. Rusty was there sitting in a lounge chair at the fire place and talking to Luke and Brian.

"I have just learned that Luke was in his third year as an apprentice carpenter and Brian has said he sees no reason why he should not complete his qualifications over the next few months when he has had time to access his work knowledge and skills."

"How do you feel about that Luke, does that sound okay with you?" queried John.

"Sure, at the moment I feel like I am in limbo with not having finished my apprenticeship, I know it is only a bit of paper and it does not mean very much in today's changed climate, but all my life I have always wanted to be a carpenter, the same as my dad was before me."

"Great, you know you are more than welcome to be here with us in the village, you are now one of us and are very welcome."

At that moment Adam and Sarah arrived in through the front door and joined them in the lounge and Sarah's eyes were sparkling with delight as she stood in the lounge holding Adam's hand. "I just love the cottage that you have allocated us, it is perfect and it is full of antique period furniture that just fits in perfectly with the design of the house."

"You are both more than welcome and I think you will find that at the back of the house that the wood shed is fully stocked with cut wood for your fire and also for the stove and oven in the kitchen."

At that moment Hal, Alice and Peter arrived in through the front door and were again introduced around the gathering that was quickly getting to standing room only in the lounge. Several of those in the lounge started to drift into the dining room with beers in their hands and claiming a seat there for themselves. Soon all twenty eight villagers new and old were seated in the dining room and Mary and Rosemary were serving up the food, helped by the three girls.

After lunch most of the village stayed in close proximity to the lounge and dining room so as to be able to here the news from the trip and what adventures had befallen them. After an hour had passed John and Rusty seemed to stand as if in unison and declared that all the new stores had to be packed away before it got dark, so everyone filed outside and started to unload the four Range Rovers first before they tackled the large van. All the food items were unpacked and stored away and then the clothing items until eventually there were only the medical items to be unpacked and stored in the house that was now a fully functional surgery and hospital. Hal and Elizabeth as their trainee doctor and qualified pharmacist were duly impressed by the range of equipment and drugs they had brought back with them from their trip to London. Anne was there as well as their nurse to help pack everything away. By the time that darkness had fallen everything had been put away into its proper place and added to the appropriate list.

Adam and Sarah along with Peter were issued with stores to stock their larders and freezersp that they packed away as well before their tea. The meal was not quite as crowded as lunch had been as a few couples had elected to dine in their own homes. It was explained to the newcomers that it was purely at their own discretion if they ate at the house or in their homes, it all depended on their mood at the time. At tea time John asked if anything had happened while they were away and was told that two more couples were expecting babies, Tom and Mary and Mike and Elizabeth.

John asked was there something in the water or was he living in a village of sex maniacs and was bombarded with crusts of bread and anything else the four sets of parents could grab and throw at him before he escaped into the kitchen and cowered behind Mary for protection

Their new doctor who was present during the altercation spoke up and asked when the four sets of babies were due and was told two of the babies were due in August and the other two were due in October.

"Well seeing as it is now the beginning of April perhaps in the morning if the four sets of parents would like to visit him at the surgery he would talk to them and check their health and the babies as his first acts as the village doctor and if Anne could find time to act as his nurse during the consultations he would be grateful and if the new parents wouldn't mind Hal should be there as well as his intern to start him on to the road of learning so that he could eventually qualify as a doctor as well. The first appointment was set up for ten o clock so as tho give him some time to sort out the surgery a bit more to the way he liked things. After tea everyone by mutual consent headed home to their individual homes for the night as everyone was tired from unloading the supplies and repacking them all away again into their respective places of storage.

The next morning Anne was the first to arrive at the surgery and found that Peter had placed chairs in the hallway for potential patients to sit on while waiting and had sorted out the consulting room which used to be the dining room and organised it the way he wanted it. One of the bedrooms he had made into a two bed ward using the proper hospital beds that they had brought back to the village and stored in the surgery. Another bed room he had started to set up as an operating theatre complete with autoclave and instrument trolley and another bedroom was already set up as a storage room for all the medicines and spare equipment The lounge he had kept for himself as his residential lounge and that left him the last bedroom for himself.

"Hi Anne I am starting to feel organised at last and I must say quite excited, just like I was when I first started into practice about ten years ago."

"What on earth time were you up at this morning to get this much done."

"Oh I don't really know it seem only a few minutes ago because I have been so busy. One thing I have noticed that we require badly are some theatre lights for the operating room and an independent supply of power so that we do not have any failure during a procedure, that could be catastrophic "

"Yes I agree it is something that we have forgotten about are the lights, I will show you the find it shopping list we keep up at the main house for adding any items to that someone wants. At that moment their first patient arrived, it was Joanne and her partner Brian. Peter asked them if they would come into his examination room along with Anne as the resident nurse. The examination went without a hitch and he agreed that the baby was due on the eleventh of August after seeing the baby on the Ultra Sound which Anne was able to operate although she was the first to admit that she was not qualified to operate the machine as she was not a radiologist, but she and Peter between them were able to pool their knowledge and work it successfully.

The parents to be were told that everything looked good and that the mothers health was good and they were given a book to read on birthing and asked to share it with one of the other sets of parents as they only had two of that particular book available and Peter made a note of the title so as to put a few more of them on to the to get list. By the time it came to show them out of the surgery two more sets of potential parents had arrived and were sitting in the chairs in the corridor. The next set of parents to be were Beth and Mike who after the examination were told that their baby should be due on the eight of October and again they managed to use the Ultra Sound successfully, again mother and baby were doing good and Peter told them to share the book that he had give to Joanne and Brian. Next were Mary and Tom who again Peter was able to confirm that the baby was due on the third of August. The last couple were Alice and Hal whose baby was determined to arrive on the eighteenth of October and was perfect but that Alice 's blood pressure was slightly elevated but not enough to worry about but she should be careful not to overdo anything and no lifting of any heavy objects and no alcohol and she should, make an appointment every week until the birth so that he could keep an eye on things but she really had no reason to worry as everything else was good and she had one main thing going for her and that was her age as she was only twenty five years of age going on twenty six, he gave her the other book he had on birthing. After the talk he had with Alice he had a conversation with Hal and Anne and asked them how they thought the examinations had gone, both expressed their delight on the way things had gone and agreed that they should keep an eye on Alice but to keep it unobtrusive so as not to alarm her and they also explained a bit about what they knew of Alices history and the way she had been abused in the past. Peter made notes on the file he had started for her and explained that a patients notes should be self explanatory so that if another doctor was to take over a patient the notes would completely fill him in on all aspects of the patient and should not be notes that only he understood. He looked over the notes he had made on the other three files as well and added a couple of things where he felt that he had not sufficiently explained himself.

"Well I think that is it folks, our first surgery seems to be over and all the patients are doing well, thank you for your help."

Hal and Anne said their goodbyes to Peter and made their way back to the main house and arrived just in time to hear John and Rusty setting up the first party for the year to go out and cut up logs for the village and also they were organising another couple of people to go out and see how the grass was growing in the fields where they cut the hay later on when it had reached its maximum growth potential.

Brian and Luke were discussing about going into Holt to get some good timber to make another couple of cots for the expectant mothers and also to bring back other timber that they may find a use for other jobs as they came up. Those that had gone out to look at the growth of the hay returned and said it was looking good and they should be able to cut it probably by the end of next month or the beginning of June.

The log cutting party returned at four o clock before dusk and unloaded their load of cut logs around the individual houses first. After tea that night Tom was sitting at the radio with his ear phones on fiddling when he got excited and shouted that he had got something. The CD that was playing was hurriedly shut off and he unplugged the ear phones so that everyone could hear what was coming over the short wave radio. After a few minutes of fine tuning they were able to hear a male voice asking was there anyone out there. Tom spoke into his microphone.

"I hear you this is Tom Fielding from Norfolk returning your call, can you hear me?"

A reply came back practically immediately.

"Yes, yes I can this is Bob Hammersley from Manchester, we have only just managed to get the radio to work and are delighted to know that there are other people out there, how many of you are there?"

"We have managed to gather together a community of thirty people men, women and children. How many in your group?"

"There are seven of us, three men two women and two children both boys. You seem to have done better than us in gathering together a group."

"We have only just had an exploration party return from London and on down to Southampton and they brought back another five people just this week. We are practically sure that there are no more people out there in southern England, but we have not explored Wales at all yet."

"We have explored north to Leeds and south to Wolverhampton but not the surrounding countryside so there is possibly some more people out there in the smaller towns and villages, we thought that we would do another trip of exploration before the summer is over and see if we had any luck in finding anyone else. I would have thought that you would have found more people in London because of its size."

Tom explained that they had found a group of four men who had been keeping women as slaves and they had to dispatch with them and the women were now part of their community and another man in London had gone mad and had killed a couple of other people before someone else managed to kill him so that was a potential seven people that should have been alive and well and with them but unfortunately were not. The conversation went back and forwards for the rest of the night before they signed off and agreed to get back to each other the following evening.

After Tom had signed off there was great excitement with everyone discussing the other group and wondering how they had managed to survive and if the dog packs and rats were a problem with them too.

Everyone had a lot to talk about before they went to bed that night. The next morning six of the men went out to the forest where they were cutting logs for the winter, by the end of the day they had managed to cut enough logs to fill both the flat bed trucks to capacity. When they arrived back at the village they again went to the private houses first to stock them to capacity before stocking the main house. After unloading all the logs they went into the main house and had a few beers before sitting down to tea, after tea Tom went back on to the radio to talk to the other group in Manchester. They talked for the rest of the evening and passed information back and forth on different things they had done to survive. Tom had mentioned that they were looking for a larger generator for the mill to give them the ability to generate more electricity and Bob Hammersley happened to mention that there was a firm in Manchester that manufactured generators and turbines and the next time they got a chance they would call in and see what they had that might be suitable for their needs. They also mentioned that where they were just outside Manchester they had noticed an increase in the rat population and after hearing their story that they might have to do something about their defences for the coming winter. Tom suggested that they visit an army barracks and see if they could get a hold of some flame-throwers similar to what they had managed to get, and to set up some sort of defence that involved surrounding themselves with a ditch of flames. They continued to chat for a while and decided to set up a fixed time of seven in the evening to contact each other on a regular basis.

They signed off the radio and a few of the men decided to have a game of cards. They had become a bit more sophisticated now because someone had found boxes of chips at the toy shop at the last visit and they were able to use them as markers when playing poker or a few of the other card games. Gradually the main house emptied as people started to head home to their beds because they had to get back into the log cutting in the morning.

The next morning after one of Mary's breakfasts they headed back to the woods. They stopped for lunch and had the packed lunch that Mary had put together for them that consisted of coffee. soft drinks, some sandwiches, home baked buns and tarts and some apples that were left over from their scrumping through an orchard somewhere. Not long after they had started there was a yell of pain from Mike Thornton who was operating one of the chain saws. When they ran over to him they saw he was lying on the ground holding his lower leg and screaming with the pain. When cutting through a tree the saw had slipped and grazed across his lower leg, it seemed to have cut him into the bone at the side of his right calf., there was blood everywhere.

Hal who was there working with them got a compression bandage from the first aid kit and applied it along with a tourniquet. With everyone helping they got him up onto one of the flat bed trucks that they hadn't loaded with any logs yet and with two men on the back with him supporting him from rolling about they headed back to the village as quickly as they could.

They arrived at the gate and sounded their horn several times urgently and Rusty came running out of the house and up the road to them, he shouted.

"What's wrong?"

John who was one of those on the back of the truck supporting Mike quickly told him as he was opening the gate.

"The Doc. is in his house at the moment, head straight over to the surgery."

They drove straight over to the front door of the surgery and someone opened the front door that was unlocked because no one locked their doors anymore in the village.

They carried him inside and straight to the room that was used as an operating room and the doctor who had heard the commotion came out of his lounge and saw it was something serious with all the blood that was to be seen. He was quickly filled in with the details and said could someone get Anne as he was going to need her along with Hal who was already present as he had come back to the village with the patient.

Perter said to Hal. "Would you cut off his pants while I get myself ready." As he turned to a side trolley and rolled up his sleeves and pulled on a gown and poured alcohol over his hands before putting on gloves. "Sorry but I don't have time to wash my hands the alcohol will do the trick instead, right Hal can you clean yourself up and put on a gown and gloves and I will start to clean the wound to see how it is. Can you prepare a syringe of morphine for me please Hal, the rest of you I will have to ask you to leave now thank you and he indicated the door with a turn of his head.

By this time Mike was unconscious from the loss of blood and the pain of his wound.

Peter was into the wound and had found the main artery that was severed and clamped it off while he explored the rest of the wound. Anne arrived and without being told put on a gown and gloves after using the trick with the alcohol to sterilise her hands. A woman's raised voice could be heard outside the door so presumably Beth had arrived and was anxious to come in but was being restrained.

"He is very lucky that the saw grazed along his leg and did not cut the actual bones themselves, his main problem is loss of blood, when I rejoin his artery I will take a sample of his blood and see what type it is and then we can pray that someone in the village is the same type as him."

After cleaning up the wound and stitching up the gash in his leg he turned to Hal who was already checking his blood type with a microscope in the surgery.

"Here we are he is lucky he is type O+ and someone of us already here must be the same with the law of averages." He went outside and asked those present if they knew what blood type they were. Two of those in the hall were type O+ and he brought them inside to the operating room and chairs for them to sit on and set up to take blood from the two volunteers. Hal worked with one and Anne started with the other one who happened to be Mike's partner Beth and they proceeded to take some blood from them both. The minute the first bag was half full Peter brought it over to Mike and connected it to his arm to transfuse it and Hal connected another bag to Joanne and said it is that good we have decided to bottle it so we are going to drain you, you don't mind do you?"

Joanne smiled and said. "Take whatever you want."

"I am only joking it is just that I had to stop half way before because I was anxious to get some blood back into him as quickly as possible."

Soon they had the two extra bags of blood and Peter said that he would be surprised if that was not enough to do the job.

They carried him gently into the bedroom that had been made into a double ward and put him to bed.

"He will sleep now for a while and he should be okay, nothing that a week of rest on his back won't fix, Beth if you want to sit quietly with him I will make you a cup of tea and you can rest after both the shock and the giving of blood. Joanne I want you to sit and rest until I get a cup of tea into you as well." Peter left the ward and bustled into the kitchen and put on the kettle. Anne meantime was cleaning up the mess in the operating room and getting it back to a spic and span condition. Everyone else was sent home and Peter told them he would be okay and he would keep them all posted as to his condition.

The log cutting team went back to the woods to finish loading up the second truck with the cut logs. When they stopped work at the end of the day they delivered the logs around the village. They reckoned that another day would see all the houses stocked up and then they would concentrate on the main house.

At tea Peter announced that the patient was doing well and maybe someone could bring some food to the surgery for both the patient and Beth who was still sitting with him. The girls volunteered to bring the food down the street to the surgery.

The next morning the wood cutting team went back to carry on with the task and get it finished and by that night they had cut enough logs to completely restock the wood shed of the main house and some left over as well. The doctor spent the evening going round everyone in the village asking them all what their blood type was and those that did not know he made an arrangement for them to come to the surgery the next morning to be tested and be blood typed. This way in future he would know what everyone's blood type was and there would not be any delay trying to find out.

Also he had a word with all four of the mothers to be and suggested that they start before the due date giving some of their own blood so he had a stock on hand in case anything went wrong during the delivery, he felt it was better to be safe than sorry, all agreed that they would do it. As blood can only be stored for forty two days under suitable refrigeration, he would like to harvest two litres from each prospective mother starting about thirty days before the due date of the babies, not that two litres was the be all or end all, it was better than nothing if anything went wrong.

Over the next week the doctor went around everyone in the village and obtained their blood types and complete medical histories as far as everyone was able to remember.

Mike was kept in bed in the surgery for the next two days, complaining all the time that he was well enough to go home and be looked after by Beth, who had hardly moved from his side for the two days. Eventually he was allowed to go home by Peter under strict guidelines not to over exert himself for a couple of days and he was not allowed to leave his home for the next forty eight hours and after that short walks out to his front gate or back garden until he got some strength back into the injured leg. After about a week he was able to hobble with the help of a walking stick up to the main house but still had to be careful not to overdo it. Eventually the day dawned when he was able to have the stiches removed all fifteen of them. Peter explained why there were so many stiches was because the chainsaw had skidded down his leg before it had finally bitten into the leg tissue and chipped the bone. He was told that he would probably have a certain amount of pain from arthritis because the actual bone had a few millimetres of bone chipped off down its length although through time it should grow back but may leave some residual effects.

CHAPTER 11

GETTING READY FOR THE THIRD WINTER.

The following week it was decided to send a scavenging party to Holt and Peter asked could he go with the group as he wanted to collect some things for the surgery.

They set off with a panel van and a flat bed truck. When they arrived in Holt they went first to the local hospital and Peter supervised the removal of a set of theatre lights and another instrument trolley and he also gathered up a couple of sets of crutches and walking sticks and then he went to the red cross laboratory and obtained the necessary equipment for taking blood and cleaning it up and also for taking and separating plasma and a couple of boxes of empty blood bags. His next call was to the dental department and he took a dentists chair and a complete selection of instruments and any books on dentistry that he could find, he was the first to admit that he knew next to nothing about dentistry but he thought that it was likely that someone was going to need the services of a dentist in the future.

After Peter had filled his immediate list of requirements the others headed for the farm produce wholesalers and stocked up with animal feeds for their small stock of varied animals on the farm. They also collected a supply of fertilisers suitable for the growing of vegetables in their expanding vegetable garden and of course the usual tins of food items for the stock room.

They got back to the village in the early afternoon and after unloading the food items and the items for the farm they headed down to the surgery and with the help of their resident electrician Tom they installed the theatre lights and dentists chair and then left Peter to fiddle about installing all the items he had acquired for the taking of blood and the cleaning and storage of it, they also installed for him a special fridge that would be used for storing blood and specific vials of medications that should be stored in a fridge.

At dinner that evening Peter professed to be satisfied that he had most of the equipment required for most emergencies.

The weather was bright and sunny and not a cloud in the sky which was perfect for the eighteenth of June. It was decided that they would on the next day head out to the field ear marked for hay gathering and start cutting the hay and make the most of the good sunny weather. By the end of two weeks they reckoned that they had enough hay cut to last them through the winter, they also had cut some coarser grass that could be used for the bedding of the animals. Over the next week they gathered the hay and coarser grasses and by the end of the month had the cut hay and raised it into stooks which by the end of the month was gathered up and stored in bales into the storage sheds at the farm.

At the village meeting at the end of June John and a couple of the others expressed their concerns about the pools of expertise that they had in the village and the many gaps that there were, actually there were more gaps than anything else in their pool of knowledge. They had a surgeon, medical doctor, carpenters, electrician, building, surgical, pharmaceutical, nursing, engineering, schooling, computer technician and Bobbie for farming, but when you listed the qualifications out in a list it showed the gaps that there were and no endless resource pool to draw from, because civilisation as they all knew it had ceased to exist much as it was an unpleasant fact that had to be faced.

One suggestion was to ask the group they had contacted in Manchester would they like to join their group in the village, also should they mount another expedition before the winter arrived to see if they could find any one else out there to the West into Wales and the North West of England towards the Manchester group. Everyone in the village thought that these ideas were good and it was decided to put them to a vote as they still had five unoccupied houses in the village that would take another five couples. Another suggestion that came up was to build another couple of bedrooms to be attached on to the main house.

A vote was taken on each item discussed and it was decided to explore these options immediately, starting with putting forward the amalgamation of the two groups that evening when the talked on the radio to the Manchester group. They decided not to lose any more time and to send into Holt a couple of trucks to gather up supplies necessary to build the two bedroom extension on to the main house and get it underway immediately The two carpenters Brian and Luke and also Jason the handy man and builder felt they could easily manage the construction of the extension and Tom could do the wiring and they would send out two expeditions who would be Adam and Sarah and Peter and Jean and John and Anne would go north to meet the Manchester group half way and guide them in the rest of the way. Mike and Beth would go out with the largest panel van and just look for and bring back food items only. Rusty, Don and Joseph would go back out and get stuck into more wood gathering and this time they would try and cut enough logs to completely fill the wood sheds of the five unoccupied houses in the village even if they were not going to be filled it was thought a good idea to get it done once and for all and some of the women left in the village could help with the stacking and unloading of the cut logs.

That evening after they had made contact on the radio John approached the group in Manchester and put to them the suggestion that they would be more than welcome to join their group here in the village and explained their reason for making the suggestion as they would like to gain their skills into the village pool of skills as a means of building up civilisation once more for the future and the advantages they could offer the other group was security, medical and a well organised home base to belong to with other people sharing the load of survival and day to day living. He said that they could take as long as they wanted to discuss the possible situation and all the ramifications as they would apply to them. He also explained that they were sending out two more exploration teams to see if they could find anyone else before winter set in and what areas they had thought of exploring. Also that he understood that in the Manchester group they had two couples and they had five house left in the village that were unoccupied that they could take their pick from.

He had only stopped speaking when he heard a laugh come over the radio and Bob Hammersley replied that they would not require any time to make up their minds as they had already discussed the possibility with each other and were going to ask could they join their group in Norfolk, so the answer was a definite yes and they would start packing up their possessions and would be ready to leave by the end of the week.

"That is great." Replied John. "We will send a party to meet you along the way once we have decided the route that you will take so that we don't miss each other." They chatted for another thirty minutes and went over the main plans of what they needed to do and what the other party from Manchester would bring with them so as not to bring items that were not required

By the end of June the different expeditions were ready to get under way.

Already the guys that were doing the extension had laid the foundations and had poured the concrete for the slab for the extension and had made a couple of trips into Holt for building materials and were hard at work. Anyone that could be spared gave their services to the building project even if it was only grunt tasks that required no special skills but it all helped at the end of the day.

The morning of the first of July dawned and the three expeditions set off on their various allotted tasks. Initially they would travel in convoy as far as

Peterborough when on reaching it John and Anne would break off and head north towards Rotherham and hopefully meet the party from Manchester along the way, but they would not go any further north than the southern approach road into Rotherham because they did not want to miss the party coming south.

The other two vehicles would stay together until they reached Leicester and there they would part as one vehicle went further west towards Wolverhampton and Birmingham and the other vehicle would turn towards Coventry. It was decided that if they found anyone they would try and get them to head back to the village on their own if possible if they decided to join their group at the village. It had been decided that no party should stay away for longer than a month.

When they reached Leicester John and Anne said their good byes and turned north for Rotherham. The roads were in remarkably good condition especially from Leicester to Rotherham as they were mostly travelling on motorways and other than the odd vehicle that had crashed or just pulled into the edge of the road there were no obstructions worth speaking off. They did not have to use their chain saws once. The hundred miles to Leicester had taken them eight days with three vehicles of people helping to clear the road. From there the hundred miles north to Rotherham had only taken one day and when they arrived they found a convoy of three vehicle waiting for them outside the city on the southern approach road they were travelling on. There was one large truck with a canvas covered load on top of it and one land cruiser and one panel van. The pulled up beside the other vehicles and got out and went over to meet the new comers that were going to the village.

"Hi I am John and this is my partner Anne, welcome, it is good to see you, I hope you had an uneventful trip so far."

"Hi I am Bob and this is my partner Judy and this is Phillip and his partner Susanne and this is Arthur and of course these are the two boys, Phillip who is fifteen and Austin who is eleven. We are delighted to meet you at last and thank you very much for asking us to join your group, the ladies especially will be a lot more reassured and feel more secure, the dog packs are pretty bad up our way but the rats have not been to bad so far they are just starting to make their presence felt and being seen in larger groups."

I vote that we camp here for the night if you have no objection and then set off early in the morning. You seem to have brought everything including the kitchen sink with you." replied John as he indicated the lorry with its tarp covered load

"Actually that is a present from us to you at the village for taking us in, you had mentioned that you were looking for a larger generator and turbine and that is what that is, we had gone looking after you had mentioned it to us and found what we hope will do the trick for you as along as we can use a crane or some such thing to unload it as it is quite heavy, we had a job getting it loaded on to the truck and had to use a crane."

"You are not serious, are you? I have a couple of people in the village and they will have raptures when they see it. You have certainly brought your welcome with you."

They made camp and organised a rota of sentries for the evening because of the dog packs which they were told were pretty bad.

The next morning after a hot drink as no one was in the mood for delay they set off back south heading for their turn off point at Leicester which they reached in just over two hours and decided to keep going until they reached Peterborough and then to stop there for the night and try and do the next part of the trip in a couple of days, because of the work they had already done in clearing the road. They reached Peterborough and stayed the night in a hotel and barricaded themselves in. The next morning they headed of on what they hoped would be the last leg of their journey home. They arrived at the village just as dusk was falling and drew up at the gate and were spotted by Rusty who was standing outside the front door of the main house just admiring the fall of the evening. He shouted into the house and ran up the road towards them and yelled a welcome to the whole party and opened the gates and let them drive in and on down to the main house where they parked and dismounted from the cabs of their vehicles and stretched their stiff bones from the trip when they dismounted.

The newcomers were brought inside and introduced to everyone that was present and probably promptly then forgot the names they had been introduced to and were seated and given a hot drink or beer as their taste dictated. The two couples were then taken down the road to see their new houses and to let them get a fire lit as soon as possible and invited back for tea. Arthur was given Paul's old room and the two boys Philip and Austin moved in with Paul into one of the new rooms that had been added on to the house and had four bunks in it. This left one bedroom in the new wing that was empty and one bunk free in both the boys room and the girls room where Martha was at present with the three girls and she had approached John and asked would he mind if she moved in with Peter Willouby over at the surgery as they had become very friendly and they both would like to move in together. John had expressed his delight and said go for it and she had moved out of the main house and in with Peter immediately.

The week after John and Anne returned there was a vehicle honking at the bridge gates and when they investigated they found a man and woman there that said they had met Adam and Sarah in Coventry w ho asked them if they would like to join the community in Hunsworth and they had accepted as they had found it hard going surviving on their own in Coventry. They had actually fortified a house on the outskirts of the city and had found the dog packs becoming very aggressive. They introduced themselves as John Braun and his partner a younger girl named June Sadler. He was twenty nine years of age and she was eighteen, she had been a shop assistant and he had been a welder and sheet metal worker in a car factory in Coventry. They were welcomed by everyone and shown to one of the remaining empty houses in the village by everyone and helped to settle in. They appeared to be very friendly and as

Mary remarked very much in love and she thought that was great being a born romantic. They said that Adam and Sarah were going to investigate the city and surrounding area before returning possibly in the next few days, because they had mentioned that they had thought there was someone else living in Coventry but could not be sure as they had never seen them.

The weather had now turned very hot as it was the middle of summer being the eight of July. They returned five days later on the thirteenth of July and said it was good to be home again.

The afternoon of the seventeenth of July Peter and Jean returned and brought with them another woman and a young boy that they had found in Wolverhampton. The woman identified herself as Barbara Bailey, she was thirty years of age and was a theme park guide for a safari park outside Wolverhampton and the young boy was twelve years of age and his name was Todd Weston and did not have very much to say, he still appeared to be traumatised from the five day sickness and loss of his parents. They moved the young boy in to the four bunk room with the other three boys and moved Don and Joseph downstairs into the new room they had just built because it was larger than the room they were currently occupying and were able to move in a couple of desks and chairs for them to work at and moved Barbara Bailey into their old room and took out one of the beds. The two new arrivals in the village meant that there were now thirty seven people living in the community and that included seventeen men, thirteen women and four boys and three girls making a total of seven children.

Because of the number of children in the village it was decided that one of the last two vacant houses would be made into a school for the seven children, they went back to the pub and eatery The Honey bell and brought back small tables that could be used as school desks and also chairs to fit out two class rooms of ten tables and chairs each and also a table for the front of the classrooms for the teacher and a chair. The next trip into one of the nearby towns they would bring back a couple of blackboards and chalk and dusters for the teachers.

Joanne Begley was asked if she would take over the task as the main teacher in charge of the children's education and Arthur Groundwater if he would teach mathematics, Mike Thornton was to teach manual arts such as carpentry and metalwork when they managed to gather in to the village the necessary equipment required including lathes and tools etc. It was also decided that they would teach the children computer sciences so that computer skills did not die out, Adam Dundass and Susanne Richards were roped in to teach these skills to the children. None of these suggestions or preparations were welcomed with enthusiasm by any of the children but all in the village agreed that they did not want to be raising morons for the future. There would be school lessons each day from Monday to Friday from nine in the morning until one in the afternoon.

The beginning of August arrived and the whole village were waiting expectantly for the first new arrival to be born in the village to Mary Harrington and Tom Fielding due on the third day of August. Right on cue Mary went into labour on the second of August at ten o clock at night and was moved into the surgery with the doctor assisted by Hal and Anne standing by in readiness. The baby arrived without any complications at three in the morning and the word was passed that both mother and baby were doing well. Mary and the baby girl stayed in the surgery for another day and night and were then allowed home to their own house.

The next mother to be did not wait for her due date of the eleventh of the month but went into labour on the ninth of August and gave birth that evening to another baby girl and again there were no complications and were duly allowed home after another night in the surgery.

They were now into the middle of August and life in the village settled down into a well run routine, they still tried the radio every evening but still they had no other success in that area. On one of the trips into the major towns they picked up over a dozen new computers and several printers and other computer hardware and software including the Encyclopaedia Britannica that their two resident experts and other teaching staff said they needed and installed a computer room for the students and also put one into the Doctors surgery and gave one along with a printer to Arthur for him to work on in his bedroom for whatever a mathematician required a computer for.

They also brought back a forklift and a mobile crane to the village to help lift the generator and turbine into position at the mill. They needed the crane too lift the generator off the flat bed truck that it had arrived on and also the turbine which itself was weighty. They used the forklift to carry the generator into the mill through the double doors at the end of the building that had originally been used by horses and carts to bring the grain into the mill for milling. This still left a lot of brute force to be used along with pulleys and chains to get them into position with a lot of manpower being used as well. It was then up to the electricians and engineers to put it together and make it work, they were hopeful that it would be up and running before winter set in.

They were now coming to the end of September and the days and evenings were getting colder and it was decided to once again slaughter some of the animals from the farm for the use of the community which had grown over the last year and meat was now a scarce item on the menu at meal time. They singled out one of the bullocks and three of the pigs and two of the sheep. They had decided to increase the number of animals slaughtered because nature had been good and the birth rate with the livestock had been good and they now had a lot more animals than they originally had started with and they may even do another slaughter in the middle of next year. The hens they decided to leave until closer to Christmas. They started with the bullock and found the system of hooks and pulleys they had installed at the end of last year made the job so much easier. The beast was soon dispatched and gutted and they cut it up into the various sections of meat as per the butcher's chart showing the different cuts of meat and where they were located on the different beasts, cattle, pigs and sheep, that they had acquired and put up on a wall in the slaughter shed. When the meat was cut up it was packed into the forty litre plastic storage boxes they had used previously for this task and loaded onto one of the flat bed trucks and carried back to the main house for Mary to pack away. The slaughter of the pigs and sheep went ahead without incident and they were cut up as well and loaded onto the truck and transported to the house. All the knives and tools were cleaned, sharpened and oiled and then put away for the next time and the floor of the shed was hosed out and everything left clean before they locked the shed.

On the next trip into Holt they brought back another kit for a prefabricated shed that could be used as a garage for servicing their growing fleet of vehicles. The concrete slab was poured at the end of the village next to the mill and the shed was erected and they acquired a hoist for lifting the vehicles and all the tools required by a mechanic for servicing or repairing their vehicles. Their wisdom of keeping the majority of their vehicles all the same make now paid off that when collecting spares they only had to gather up what was required for mainly range rovers.

Because of the numbers now living in the village they were making more frequent trips scavenging for food. All the closest shops in the adjacent villages and hamlets were by now completely stripped of anything useful and they were having to go further a field to satisfy their shopping expeditions.

The next birth due on the eight of October was suddenly upon them when Beth went into labour on the morning of the eight of October and was still in labour by ten o clock that evening. And the doctor had to induce labour and found that when the baby was born there was a complication of the cord being around its neck, but luckily both came through the experience with flying colours and the spare blood stored was not required, she was made to stay in the ward for two nights before being let home because the doctor wanted to keep an eye on them both. Mike was absolutely thrilled to bring his partner and baby boy home to the nursery that they had made for the new arrival.

After the birth of Beth's baby John and Anne announced that they were expecting as well and the baby was due at the start of next summer in May, on the fourth.

The next birth being looked forward too was Alice and Hal due on the eighteenth. Alice was very nervous even though she had no problem with possible high blood pressure that had been picked up at the start of her pregnancy by the doctor. She went into labour early on the sixteenth and gave birth to a beautiful baby girl without any problems at all and was allowed home the next day.

November dawned with a hard frost but still no snow and the men checked their defences along the complete boundary both at the field fencing and the river bank and found everything to be in order and there were no last minute panics. The new generator and turbine was switched on at last on the seventh of November and found to work perfectly and the output of electricity had more than doubled and they were able to have electricity connected to the school and that meant that they were able to operate the computers that had been installed there and also the lathes etc.

They also fed the power into the grid system protecting their defences that it could be diverted over to it if required by just flicking a switch. The rat population had been discouraged through out the year by shooting any rats to be seen on the far riverbank and also by sending out shooting expeditions with shotguns to kill any that were to be found for up to a mile around the village. Unfortunately they were being seen with more frequency now that winter was on the way so it was decided that every day they would send out the two flat bed trucks with shooters on the back to see if they could decimate the population any and stop them gathering into the hoards that had appeared the previous year. They must have literally killed hundreds of them but when they went back to the village they just returned again. They sent out the larger panel van on its last shopping expedition and several of the ladies wanted to visit Kings Lynn toy shop and a few other shops for Christmas presents so another couple of the rovers accompanied the expedition for the last trip of the season before the snow arrived and closed the roads. While the ladies searched the shops for whatever goodies they wanted they backed the van up to the loading dock of one of the supermarkets and proceeded to load it to the top with cartons of food items that they thought may be the best for storage purposes. The men also visited a couple of gun shops and stocked up on shotgun cartridges to replace the ones they had expended on the rat population on their hunting trips. They had already replaced the canisters for the flame throwers

After several hours they were all ready to return home with the goods they had liberated from the shops. After an uneventful trip back they arrived at the village safe and sound. Meal time at the main house with winter on its way seemed to act as an encouragement for the numbers to increase although the four sets of new parents were not to be seen as often as previously as was to be expected. Mary was of course expecting a full turnout of everybody for Christmas dinner and no excuses would be accepted. As well as the new parents having play pens in their own homes for the babies one slightly larger one had appeared in the lounge of the main house so that when any of the parents appeared with their babies they could be put safely into the playpen and let the parents relax a bit and socialize with their friends.

The children were looking forward to Christmas morning and those that had been there for the previous couple of Christmases had wired up the new arrivals of what they could possibly expect. The Christmas decorations had suddenly appeared and the house was looking very festive and the men had gone out and selected a fir tree that the children had spent a compete morning decorating it and for the first time they had some electricity to spare and they had even managed to put some Christmas lights on it.

The first scurry of snow arrived during the night of the fourteenth of December but it was only a light fall and did not last long on the ground before it disappeared. The rats did not seem to be making any move towards attacking the village but they had instigated the usual patrols twenty four hours a day and switched on the flood lights at night along the perimeter of the fencing and facing across the river. On Christmas Eve the children all hung their stockings from the mantle shelf above the fireplace. They were all sent off packing to bed early although they could still be heard wrecking around and playing in their rooms for quite a while and had to be shouted at to go to bed or Santa Clause may not come. The adults all stayed up late and drank to much brandy and other spirits.

The next morning when they got up it was a beautiful picture postcard morning with the snow finally arriving in force and it was already over a foot deep. The patrols reported that for some reason the rats had disappeared and there was no sign of them anywhere. Bobbie and Poh had been up to the farm at dawn and the other children had been chased out to collect the eggs and milk before they would be allowed to open their Christmas presents that had appeared in their stockings and at the foot of the tree. Bobbie and Poh returned to the house to say that all the animals were taken care off and everyone sat down to a Christmas breakfast of fried eggs, bacon, fried potatoes, fried bread and toast and marmalade and tea and coffee. After breakfast everyone got stuck into opening the Christmas presents and also into the usual egg-nog well laced with brandy. The children were all excited and were playing with their new toys and the adults were getting tipsy while Mary and Rosemary along with a couple of other helpers were getting lunch ready. Eventually at one o clock lunch was served starting with chicken broth and home baked rolls followed with roast chicken and cranberry sauce and brussel sprouts and peas and carrots and mashed potatoes. Desert was the usual Christmas pudding and custard laced with the usual brandy and an abundance of wine with the meal. After lunch everyone was too full to move very far and they all collapsed into easy chairs in the lounge and watched the four babies playing in their playpen and the older children playing with their toys and continued with the good old tradition of getting tipsy.

John and Anne decide to go outside and look at the snow so they pulled on their coats and boots and walked across the road to the edge of the river and sure enough there wasn't a rat to be seen. They just stood and looked at the scenery and turned and looked at the house with the snow on the roof and eves and the lights of the Christmas tree could be seen through a window and they heard the Christmas carols playing and smiled at each other and John gave Anne a cuddle and said.

"It is not too bad a life we have made for ourselves. It is a NEW BEGINNING for us all. I just hope we do not stuff it up this time round like we did last time."

Lightning Source UK Ltd.
Milton Keynes UK
UKOW02f2359120716

278261UK00001B/95/P